"I couldn't put *Persuaded* down!! I LOVE LOVE LOVE romances and this is one of the best ones! . . . This is definitely one of my favorite books!"

—Tana

"It was, um, how do they say it? Unputdownable."

—Lei

"I've always loved Jane Austen's *Persuasion* and was really looking forward to reading this retelling. I thought the author did a great job mixing the charm from the original Persuasion into this modern retelling."

—Kathy

"I'm impressed how once again the characters and story remain true to the spirit of the Austen original, yet at the same time get a refreshingly modern facelift. . . . I really like *Persuaded*. It's one of the lighter *Persuasion* adaptations, but also one of the better ones."

—Mitch

"Persuaded is a cute love story. Jenni James did a good job with building a story that captures readers and refuses to let go."

—Ajm

"I shamefully admit it. I stayed up until 4 am reading this one. It was the best five bucks I ever spent on an ebook. . . . GAH!! SO GOOD."

—Cindy Davis

"Well done and adorable!"

—Lori

"If you're looking for a great way to introduce a friend or family member to the wonderful world of Jane Austen fan fiction (and perhaps the original works themselves!) give *Persuaded* a try. It's a delightful, clean, and fast-paced YA read that is sure to be a hit."

—Kim Denny-Ryder

"Ahhh. I love this book. The emotions it put me through. . . . Come on, everyone. This is a great read!"

—Avon Bernabe

"This young-adult retelling of my favorite Jane Austen novel is almost as good as the [original]."

—Jenny

"This is the happiest book EVER! One of the best that I have read! I am on cloud 9!"

—Ruby

"I love a good read, and I promise you that is what you will get with *Persuaded.*"

—Holly Bjelland

"You really really check out this series if you haven't already because it's well worth the read. It's quick, easy, fun, exciting, and—most of all—based on Jane Austen with a modern twist."

—Cathy

"Can I just say how much I love Jenni James and the cute way she re-tells Jane Austen stories? I just LOVE the Jane Austen Diaries . . . . If you haven't picked up one of these books, you should!"

—Deborah

"I thought this rendition of Jane Austen's *Persuasion* was amazing! . . . It kept me on edge the whole time! It was a perfect romance!"

—Jessica

Praise for *Northanger Alibi*
by Jenni James

"*Northanger Alibi* reminds us in comical, relatable ways that mythical creatures aren't always what they're cracked up to be, and that real boys can be even better."

—Eve'sFanGarden.com

"*Northanger Alibi* will have you laughing out loud at Claire's observations and dramatic responses. In a world where every teen girl is looking for her 'Edward' . . . , Claire's coming-of-age story is both timely and refreshing."

—Amanda Washington, author of *Rescuing Liberty*

"*Northanger Alibi* by Jenni James is one of the best new young adult books of the year, bringing together the lost beauty and drama of Jane Austen's novels with the hip teen culture of today. Absolutely wonderful and addictive."

—Brynna Curry, author of *Earth Enchanted*

"I fell in love with Claire and Tony the same way I fell in love with Edward and Bella in *Twilight*. *Northanger Alibi* has all the ingredients of a great love story."

—Greta Gunselman, killerromance.com

"Stephenie Meyer meets Jane Austen in this humorous, romantic tale of a girl on a mission to find her very own Edward Cullen. I didn't want it to end!"

—Mandy Hubbard, author of *Prada & Prejudice*

"*Northanger Alibi* was incredibly adorable and delightfully entertaining. Claire Hart is an exact replica of the standard crazy and young Twilight fan—gullible, obsessed and in love with the idea of vampires and werewolves actually being real. . . .

Mixing humor, romance and the ultimate crazy Twilight fan antics, this book will have you giggling from start to finish!"

—Katie

"I found myself laughing out loud . . . and then crying with Claire through her struggles. Yes, it is for young adults . . . but as an adult I completely enjoyed myself too! . . . I love that it is clean and there is nothing I wouldn't want my daughter to read someday. . . . Trust me, young and old alike won't be disappointed!"

—Kari

"This is a laugh-out-loud book! You will fall in love with Claire and everything that goes with her. . . . I am glad that someone has taken my beloved *Northanger Abbey* and modernized it. . . . *Northanger Alibi* is fun, exciting, and suspenseful. . . . James has hit the nail on the head with this one!"

—Keyth A. Pankau

"This a is fun, smart, funny story. . . . I couldn't put it down . . . I loved the characters. I loved the story. In short, I just plain loved this book!!"

—Candi

"A very funny, very modern remake of Jane Austen's *Northanger Abbey.* I LOVED it!"

—Laura

"*[Northanger Alibi]* is a laugh-out-loud kinda book! . . . You won't be able to stop the pages from turning!"

—Tiffany

Praise for *Pride & Popularity* by Jenni James

"This book was unputdownable. I highly recommend it to any fan of Jane Austen, young or old. Impatiently awaiting the rest of the series."

—Jenny Ellis, Jane Austen Society of North America

"*Pride & Popularity* is a delightful romantic comedy that will tug on the heartstrings of ladies—regardless of their age. . . . The fast-paced storyline will draw you in while the characters enchant you. . . . If you're looking for a refreshing reminder of how young, innocent love can break through even the most prideful of prejudices, you don't want to miss this one."

—Amanda Washington, author of *Chronicles of the Broken*

"This was an absolutely captivating read from the very first page. . . . I bought into every twist and turn and couldn't wait for Taylor and Chloe to actually get it together enough to become a couple."

—Shanti Krishnamurty, author of *Maid of Sherwood*

"Loved this book. . . . Loved the heroine—she was fiesty and funny. . . . All in all, a very good read. "

—AJ Cole, author of *The Scarmap*

"Jenni James pulled me both into the story and into Chloe's hillarious predicaments, making me forget I've been out of high school for years. . . . Readers of all ages and circumstances will find themselves falling in love with Taylor, while laughing at Chloe's reactions to him."

—Andrea Pearson, author of *The Key of Kilenya*

"One of the best remakes of *Pride and Prejudice* ever!"

—Jinx

"Dip into this excellent read and discover how relevant these Austen rewrites are for a modern-day audience. The author has achieved that incredibly impressive and nigh-on-impossible feat—she's made one of the classic novels of our time entirely her own. Read and prepare to be swept away."

—Drew Cross, author of *BiteMARKS*

"Pride & Popularity is freaking A-MAZ-ING!"

—im-reading-here

"I love this book! I fell in love with Chloe right away! . . . This is a must-read."

—Tiffany

"I just absolutely love this story!! Eeep!! <3 <3 <3"

—Rachiee

"This was the best book I've ever read on [Wattpad]!!! So freaking good. And what was really cute is that it was sort of innocent and not like a trashy they-sleep-with-each-other-every-other-chapter kinda book."

—Christyfanning

"I couldn't stop reading. It's AMAZING!"

—just_smile22

"This is so flippin' cute."

—Sweetly Southern

The Jane Austen Diaries

Pride & Popularity
Northanger Alibi
Persuaded
Emmalee

The Jane Austen Diaries

EMMALEE

JENNI JAMES

Inkberry Press, LLC
110 South 800 West
Brigham City, Utah 84302

ISBN: 978-0-9838293-8-6

To Emalee and Angela, lively and wonderful twins.
How I love you! How I miss you!

And to Jerry, my first knight in shining armor—
and the best dancing one, too!
Thank you for all the times you still save me.

ACKNOWLEDGEMENTS

I would like to thank my Heavenly Father for all the wonderful stories he has given me. Without him, I would be just a girl staring at a blank computer screen. Thank you! Thank you! God is so good to me. And thanks to my seven children and family, who put up with my constant writing and touring. Thank you for your support and for thinking I'm a cool mom. I love you so much!

Also, a great big thank you to Walnut Springs/Inkberry Press. You have brought my babies to life—you have done well. Thank you!

AUTHOR'S NOTE

In the Jane Austen Diaries, *Northanger Alibi* comes after *Emmalee* in sequence of events. We brought out *Northanger Alibi* earlier because of its Twilight theme. *Emmalee* introduces you to a younger and more naive Claire Hart. Because of what happens near the end of this book, her personality changes dramatically, and we see the new and improved Claire in *Northanger Alibi*. Do not give up on her as you read *Emmalee*. She plays the crucial role of Miss Bates from Jane Austen's original *Emma,* and sometimes she is a wee bit irritating. But as you read in *Northanger Alibi,* Claire becomes quite the heroine.

Thank you, my dear fans. I am so happy you love this series as you do. Now sit back, curl up in a nice comfy chair, and enjoy the story of Emmalee Bradford and Chase Anderson. I promise it will not disappoint!

Love,
Jenni

P.S. In chronological order, the books are *Pride & Popularity, Persuaded, Emmalee, Mansfield Ranch, Northanger Alibi,* and *Sensible & Sensational.*

ONE

♥

Never fear, milady, your knight has returned!
Which of these villains shall I behead first?

"Emmalee!" Mom's voice brought me out of my reverie.

"What?" I hollered back. Our house was pretty large. Okay, it was huge, and trying to talk to people in other parts of the house was nearly impossible. Especially since I refused to use the intercom system my stepdad had installed. Talk about so 1960s and totally embarrassing.

"Come here," was Mom's answering call. "I have some news for you."

News? Hmm. News is good. "Okay," I answered as I logged out of my account. No reason my friends should think I was a total Facebook junkie. I tried to log out regularly, just in case they thought all I did was sit in my room and surf the site. Pathetic, I know, but ever since my best friend went away to college four weeks before, Facebook was all I'd been doing. I sighed. Senior year looked like it was going to be a little bleak. I was the only one left at home now. Sometimes it stinks being the youngest.

I turned off the lights as I headed out of my bedroom. "Where are you?" I hollered into the corridor. I glanced at some of the family portraits that lined the wide hallway. My mom had commissioned an artist to paint them from old photographs.

I was determined that someday I'd be good enough to actually paint portraits myself. Of course, my favorite portrait was of me grinning adorably, sitting on a fluffy white rug slash blanket thing, in a gorgeous, ruffled yellow dress with a huge bow on my head. *How much cuter could I have possibly been?* Mom'd also had a doll made to look just like the portrait. She called it her Emma doll. It was still sitting on a shelf in my bedroom.

"I'm in the upstairs parlor, dear," Mom finally answered.

Upstairs parlor? Good grief. I turned left and followed the portraits of my ancestors—mostly from the '30s and '40s—that led to the room. Mom read a lot of Regency romance novels and liked to pretend we lived in Jane Austen's time. Hence the portrait "gallery," as she called it, and the upstairs "parlor." She originally wanted to call it the "green room" or "blue room" like they would've back in the 1800s. Thankfully, since she was constantly redecorating the room and changing the color theme, my stepdad demanded that she stick to calling it the upstairs parlor instead of changing the name every year or so.

This year, the parlor would've been called the "pink room." Shades of every color of pink, ranging from the palest blush to the darkest burgundy, were tastefully scattered around the ivory room. With plush silk accent pillows, elegant curtains, organza-covered lampshades, and artfully arranged pink knickknacks, it looked like it had come straight from the pages of *House Beautiful.* Knowing my mom, it probably did.

I paused in the doorway and looked at her. She was beautiful, strikingly so. Right then she had one perfectly manicured, diamond-ringed finger held up for me while she talked on her old-fashioned ivory-and-brass French phone. I watched as she laughed and flipped her long, smooth blonde hair. She moved the exaggeratedly curved phone receiver to the other ear and crossed her long, slim legs while she lounged on an antique cream and gold-leafed lounge chair. It had fuchsia accent pillows, of course.

Quietly, I walked into the room and sat on my favorite overstuffed chair. This year it was upholstered in a wide cream-and-rose-striped fabric. I waited a moment to see if Mom was watching before I curled my feet—shoes and all—underneath me.

"Okay, Grace. I'll let her know." Mom smiled into the phone.

Grace? She's talking to Mrs. Anderson. Hmm . . . I wonder what Taylor's mom wants. I hadn't seen him since Thanksgiving. He'd been living in Arizona the past two years while he went to college. *I wonder if he and Chloe are planning to get married or something. How long has he been going with that girl now—one year? No wait, it's been two years, hasn't it?*

"Yes. Emmalee is right here. She's going to be so happy. I can't wait to tell her." Mom smiled at me and then frowned with a pointed look at my feet.

Grudgingly, I rolled my eyes and put my feet on the floor. *She's such an Austenite!*

"Thank you so much! Tell Lionel we said hello, okay? Yes. Yes. Thanks again. Buh-bye." Mom set the phone in its cradle, her smile even more radiant than usual. "Guess what?" Her pedicured, sandaled foot gracefully slid to the floor as she sat up properly to talk to me.

I debated if I should really guess or if it was a rhetorical question.

"So are you going to guess?" Mom flashed her rings as she patted her knees.

"Taylor and Chloe Hart are finally getting married?"

"What? No, no." Mom shook her head. "You can do better than that. Think, Emmalee."

Something that will make me happy? "Can you give me a clue?"

"Fine, I'll give you one. And I swear if you don't figure it out, I may change my mind completely and not let you—"

No way! "Lady's had her puppies!"

"Yes!" Mom laughed as I ran over and threw my arms around her.

"When did she have them? Can I see them?" I was so excited, I couldn't help it. I'd been waiting for Georgia's dog to deliver her puppies for forever now.

"Yes. You can go see them. The Andersons want you to have first pick." Mom chuckled. "Now, let go before you strangle me."

I let go but then threw my arms around her again. "Thank you, Mom!"

This time she removed my limbs and held my hands in front of her. I looked down into her cheerful brown eyes and watched as they saddened for a moment.

"No more moping around, okay?" she said.

I nodded my head like I was eight instead of my newly acquired eighteen.

"I can't take it anymore. It's the one reason Dad" —Mom always called my stepfather "Dad"— "and I agreed to allow you to have a puppy. We're hoping you can be a little more pleasant around the house even though your best friend has left. It's almost the end of September and already one full month into your senior year. I want you to make the most of it, okay?"

Again I nodded, then matched Mom's rueful smile. "Sorry. Have I really been that bad?"

She grinned. "Maybe not *that* bad. Just not that good, either."

"Okay. I promise to be happier," I said. Then I added for good measure, "And I promise to find a new friend."

It worked. Mom's brilliant smile returned. "Good. You're my princess, and I want you to be happy." She squeezed my hands. "So what are you waiting here for? Go pick out a puppy."

"Yes!" After another exuberant hug and thank you, I was out of the parlor and charging down the stairs. I turned left and jogged through the formal dining room into the breakfast room, then practically skidded through the large kitchen into the mud room. Soon I was out the back door and running through our half acre of flower gardens and pathways. I barely noticed Mom's "romantic" white-trellised gazebo as I hurried to the back fence gate we shared with the Andersons.

I opened the gate and entered the splendor of their three-acre sculpture garden. No back yard in all of Farmington, New Mexico, beat this one. It was absolutely stunning. I ran down the path past the man-made lake, which was probably the size of two football fields. I shook my head at the small paddleboat and fishing pole next to the dock. *Mrs. Anderson will have a fit when she sees that.* Paddleboats and fishing line do not mesh with gorgeous floral hedges and sculptures. It reminded me of all the times Taylor and my stepbrother Zack had gotten in trouble for leaving their stuff at the dock instead of putting it back in the shed.

I rushed up the rise that led to the large, plantation-style home. Even from the back, the white mansion was simply breathtaking. I weaved around the sculptures near the covered veranda and over to the side door. I rang the doorbell and then wiped my feet while I waited for the Andersons' maid, Mrs. Little, to answer.

Just before the door swung open, I heard, "Emmalee Bradford? Is that you?"

The deep voice was most decidedly not Mrs. Little's. In fact, it belonged to one person and one person only—my knight in shining armor. I grinned. "Chase!" In less than a second, I was wrapped in the best bear hug a girl could ask for.

Taylor's older brother had been gone too long. The last time I had seen Chase was over three months ago, right before he'd headed off to Spain. I didn't realize how much I'd missed him until now. We were family—or as close to family as two neighbors who grew up together can be.

His tan face lit up with a grin. "So did you survive the summer without me rescuing you?"

I laughed and shook my head as I pulled out of his arms and stepped into his family's mud room. "Excuse me? I will have you know I am eighteen now and an adult. I'm fully capable of—"

Chase snorted and mumbled something under his breath before he said, "Really? An adult? Is that why you were tearing through the garden like a kid just a couple of minutes ago?"

What? My cheeks grew red as I sat down on the small bench and began removing my shoes. "So, I can see Spain didn't change you one bit," I said. "You're the same as you always were. I take it that's your paddleboat and fishing rod out there on the lake?"

"Dang! I forgot. Thanks." His smile grew. "Guess I need saving now, huh?"

"Probably." I rolled my eyes. "When did you get back?"

"Yesterday."

"What? Yesterday? And nobody told me?" I stood up.

He chuckled and brought his finger up under my chin, then gently turned my face from side to side.

"What?" I giggled.

He seemed baffled. "It's funny, I've never noticed how much you look like your mom."

"Really?" I beamed.

"Wow! Especially that smile. Yep, definitely just like your mom."

"Thanks."

I watched his sky blue eyes glitter for a second before he lowered his lashes. When he looked back at me, it was with his normal happy gleam. "So you're saying someone should've woke you up at nine last night and told you I had just gotten home?"

I laughed. "First off, Chase Anderson, I am eighteen, not twelve. I think the last time I went to bed at nine was when I went to Ashley Dixon's sleepover and finally zonked out at nine the next morning. Second, you left us three months ago, buddy. I wouldn't have cared if it was two o'clock in the morning, I would've expected a phone call. So, in answer to your question, yes. Come on, you're my knight. I will always be happy to see you, no matter what time it is."

"You remember that? Really?" He leaned his shoulder against the wall.

"Excuse me, but a girl does not forget the only guy who would ruin his brand-new shoes and leather coat to come save her."

"But you were ten."

"A very terrified ten-year-old girl, who Zack and Taylor refused to help and would only laugh at. Had you not come when you did—and as quickly, too—I might have drowned!"

"Well, I'm sure you remember the almost-drowning part," Chase teased. Then he added in a serious tone, "I don't think that is something any of us will ever forget." He grinned again. "I'm just surprised you remembered it was me who rescued you—and the nickname I made you call me."

"You made me?"

"Aha! Something you don't remember. It was the only thing I could think of to get you to stop crying. You were such a princess then. All girlie-girl, so I told you I was your knight coming to rescue you."

I couldn't remember, but I could imagine. Mostly I could imagine it working.

"So, you didn't run all the way up here to tell me the boat was in the lake, did you?" Chase asked.

"No. Lady had her puppies and I was coming over to see them."

"Lady? You mean Georgia's dog? Yeah, they're up in her room. Do you want me to take you up there? I'm trying to spend as much time with her as possible."

"With Lady?"

"No." He grinned again. "With Georgia. Since I've been in Spain, I have a whole summer's worth of catching up to do."

"Oh. Well, don't worry about me. I know the way."

"In that case, let me get the fishing stuff put up and then I'll see you in a minute. Georgia's not the only one I need to catch up with." Chase wiggled his eyebrows as he moved past me. In a heartbeat, he had stepped out the open door, turned the corner, and was gone.

TWO

*Have you always been this cute,
or did you have to work at it?*

"Knock, knock," I called as I tapped on Georgia's open door.

"We're back here!" a little voice rang out. "Emma, is that you?"

"Yep." I stepped into the huge playroom, which was beautifully decorated in lavender and white and full of every toy imaginable.

"Hurry—you have to see! Lady had her puppies!"

I followed the enthusiastic six-year-old's voice into the adjoining room. I looked on either side of the canopied queen-sized bed covered in white eyelet, before glancing around the rest of the pristine lavender bedroom. "Where?"

"In here! In here!" came Georgia's reply.

Just as I opened the door to her designer bathroom, I heard a giggle and mewing sounds over my shoulder. I shut the door and walked into Georgia's dressing room. "There you are!"

The little girl lay on her tummy, peering into the small, round dog bed where the Pomeranian and her brood rested.

Georgia laughed and motioned me closer, so I walked over and knelt on the floor next to her. I had never seen Lady look more proud. I raised the back of my hand for her to sniff.

"Good girl, Lady," I said. "They are simply beautiful."

All four puppies were busily nursing. Carefully, I ran one finger over the smooth back of the nearest pup.

"That's Little Lion," said Georgia. "He's my favorite."

We both began to giggle as the puppy scooted blindly over his siblings and began to search for more milk. The other puppies protested faintly as he scrambled over their heads. Georgia gently picked up Little Lion and placed him away from the rest, where he happily latched on and started to nurse again.

"Do you have names for all of them?" I asked.

"No, just Little Lion. Me and Mom decided he was the most like Dad."

I laughed. Lionel Anderson probably wasn't too thrilled to have a puppy named after him. "Were they born today?"

"Nope. Last night. It was so exciting, too! First Chase came home, and then the puppies came. Mom even let me stay up and watch."

"I bet you're tired now, huh?"

"I was, but now I'm okay. I like watching them. They're so cute."

"I can't believe how tiny they are." It looked like I could fit two puppies in the palm of my hand.

"Dr. Westbrook says they won't open their eyes for a week."

Surprised I asked, "Was she here?" The local vet very rarely made house calls.

"No, not yet. But Mom says she'll be by later this afternoon to check on them."

I wonder if the Andersons have Dr. Westbrook on speed dial. Knowing Grace Anderson, they probably did. She was meticulous when it came to details, especially when it involved her daughter.

It was no secret that Georgia was the Anderson's miracle baby. After twelve years of fertility treatments, they had given up on having another child.

"Hello, girls. Can I join you?" Chase peeked into the dressing room.

"Hi, Chase!" Georgia beamed up at him. "Come in. Emma's deciding which puppy she wants."

I moved over a bit so he could sit next to his sister. The dressing room was pretty big, but with Chase in it, it seemed much smaller.

He grinned and playfully nudged one of the puppies before looking over at me. "Have you chosen one yet?"

I smiled. "No. I'm waiting until they stop eating so I can see them better."

"Good call. You shouldn't choose today anyway— you should give them a couple weeks so you can see their personalities. Besides, right now they look more like little slugs than dogs."

"Slugs!" I chuckled and shook my head. "No way. They're adorable. I can't believe you just called them slugs."

"Don't listen to Chase," Georgia said. "He's a boy, and boys don't know anything."

"It's true." He winked at me. "I don't know anything."

I rolled my eyes and watched as the first puppy unlatched itself from its mother and curled into a ball. Lady turned and began to lick the little guy.

"So, speaking of not knowing anything," Chase said ominously, "what have you been up to?"

This oughta be good. Same old Chase. "You really should've become a police detective, you know that?" I said.

"Hey, I haven't even asked anything yet."

I grinned. "Yes. But I know it's coming."

"Okay, okay, I can take a hint. If you don't want to tell me, I'll just have to guess."

Chase leaned in and gently picked up the puppy that had fallen asleep. He stroked its petite head with the tip of his nose before he took one of my hands and placed the puppy on my palm. Lady raised her head and watched intently while I cradled the little guy next to me, but she didn't growl. After a couple of seconds, she turned and started licking another puppy.

"So, I take it you're still ruling the roost in the Bradford home?" Chase asked me.

Great. We're going this route. "What do you mean?"

"Come on, you know there's nothing your family wouldn't do if you wanted them to. You're way too spoiled for your own good."

"That's like the pot calling the kettle black, don't you think?"

"Ha! You think I've been spoiled?" Chase looked at me incredulously.

I bit my lip to hold back a smile. "Oh, Señor Español, I didn't realize life in Spain was so difficult for you."

"More difficult there for me than here for you, I am sure," Chase replied smugly.

Whatever! "I'll have you know that since Zack left, it's been really difficult, thank you very much."

"Oh, you mean you have no one to ask which fingernail polish you should choose?"

"Hey, fingernail polish is an essential accessory to any girl's outfit, so don't knock it." I laughed. "Besides, my life is not all idle, or whatever you think it is."

"Ha! I bet it is. Actually, I bet the only idle thing you don't do is *American Idol*. Never mind, I take that back. I can see by your face that you are blasé enough to actually watch that show."

"It's good! Plus, when you vote you're helping to launch someone's singing career. So therefore, you really are doing a service for America, especially if the singer is good."

"That's your idea of helping America?" Chase began to laugh—hard.

Until that moment, I never realized just how annoying laughter could be. I squinted my eyes and brought out my fake smile. "Finished?"

"Al–almost!" he gasped.

"Before you die of laughter, I'll have you know I am extremely busy helping people. In fact, in my *honors* English class, I sometimes have the privilege of tutoring the teacher."

Chase stopped laughing. "What? You tutor your teacher?"

"Well, occasionally, when Mr. Young has his facts wrong, I feel I must correct him."

"Emmalee Bradford, are you saying you correct Mr. Young?"

"On occasion, yes, Chase Anderson, I do."

"Wow! You know, that is one thing I would love to see." He shook his head and then stared at me.

"What? What are you thinking about?"

"You. Does anything phase you?"

"Of course it does," I said. "I lost my best friend this year, and that has phased me big time."

"You, lose a friend? Impossible."

Is he being sarcastic? "Well, we didn't get in a fight or anything, and she didn't die, if that's what you're thinking. She left for college."

"Ohhh." Chase nodded. "So that explains the puppy. Mom and Dad can't bear to see you mope."

"I do not mope!"

"Sure you don't."

"I'll have you know, I am, at this moment, planning on adopting someone to take Olivia's place. In—in fact, I'm thinking about picking a girl who no one would've ever noticed before and making her popular." *Now that is a good idea. I'm surprised I didn't think of it sooner.* "So there. I do plan on serving humanity."

"How? By granting some girl's wish of becoming your friend?"

"Well, yes. What's wrong with that?"

"Nothing, if you really mean to be her friend and this isn't just something to occupy yourself with until you get bored."

"Of course I mean to be her friend. I need a friend, don't I?"

Chase sighed. "Emma, I hope you know what you're doing."

"It will be perfect, you'll see. Now, enough about me. It's your turn. I want to know all about Spain. What did you do? Where did you visit? Was Spanish easier or harder for you to understand than you thought it would be?"

"Very good, Emma." Chase smiled at me. I was surprised he didn't clap. "You changed the subject as fast as any high-society matron. You mom would be very proud." He held out his hand. "No, before you get on your high horse again, I want to point out that Georgia has fallen asleep. So if you're going to say something, please try to refrain from shouting."

As if I ever shout. Urgh. Besides, I really wanted to know about Spain. I'd forgotten how quickly Chase could get on a person's nerves. I took a deep breath before whispering, "She looks absolutely adorable." Little Georgia had curled herself around the top of the basket.

"Yes, she does." Chase tenderly brushed one long strand of curly blonde hair off his sister's forehead. "When I see her, especially like this, it almost keeps me from wanting to leave again."

"Oh, are you planning to leave?"

"Eventually, yes." He turned to look at me, and his sparkling blue eyes seemed to hold a myriad of secrets.

"But why?" I asked as casually as possible. For some reason the thought of him leaving again made me feel a bit . . . sad.

"Because, Emma." He smiled a bit ruefully. "I'm twenty-one now. I can't spend my time here forever, you know."

"Oh. If you're that busy, I'm surprised you had time to come and visit your family at all." I looked away.

"Can't someone come because they miss a place?"

I caught his eyes again. "It depends."

"On?"

"On how long that person plans on staying. A week? Then no, and I wonder why he would even take the trouble. A month is decent, but not nearly enough time to—"

"How does six months sound?" Chase interrupted. He grinned as my jaw dropped.

"Six months? Really?" *That's a very long time.* I smiled back. In fact, I was probably glowing, but I didn't care.

"Are you happy now?"

"Yes."

He chuckled. "Good. And before you ask, I will tell you. I'm here to help my dad clean up a few of his businesses. I happen to be good at that."

"Cleaning up businesses?"

"Well, yeah, but I meant helping my dad."

I watched, baffled a bit, as Chase stood and walked out of the dressing room. A few seconds later, he returned with a blanket for Georgia. After he tucked the purple quilt around her, he held his hand out to take the puppy I'd forgotten I had.

"Oh, sorry." I handed the warm, sleeping body over. I smiled when Chase snuggled the puppy next to its mother. Lady immediately began to lick the little guy and welcome him back. "You did a very good job," I whispered as I stroked her soft fur. "I have never seen more beautiful puppies—ever."

I heard Chase chuckle above me. I turned and he held his hand out for me. I said a quick goodbye to Lady and then let him help me to my feet.

"Are your parents home?" I asked. "I think it's time I said hello, don't you?"

THREE

♥

So, will you give me your phone number,
or am I going to have to stalk you?

It was as I was contemplating the mysteriousness that seemed to revolve around Chase—instead of listening to Ms. Ingle during my honors history class—that I first noticed her. I asked Elton Bloomfield, the senior class president, who sat next to me, what her name was. And it took three whispered explanations before he realized which girl I meant.

"Are you talking about that weird girl sitting alone in the front of the room?" Elton asked. I could tell he was intrigued that I noticed her at all.

"Yes, with the bright yellow hobo bag. Who is she?" I quickly whispered just before Ms. Ingle turned toward us.

"I think her name is Hannah," he whispered to me once the coast was clear. "Why?"

"Because she's gorgeous. Don't you think so?"

"Gorgeous?" Clearly, Elton had never considered it before.

"Yes, look at her face. Not her hair—her face. She's really pretty."

"Well, yeah. So she's pretty. Why do you care?"

"Because I am going to make her my new best friend, that's why."

He looked shocked. "You are?"

Momentarily forgetting where I was, I laughed, earning myself a glare from Ms. Ingle. I smiled my "Bradford smile." She must've been impressed, because thankfully she didn't comment. After she turned to the chalkboard again, I thought it was safe enough to answer Elton.

"Of course, I am," I hissed. "It's going to be so much fun—I can't wait. Don't you think she'll be excited when I tell her the good news?" My eyes searched his.

"Oh, uh, yeah." He nodded. "I think so. I mean, I can't see why not. Who wouldn't want to be your friend?"

"Exactly! It's perfect, isn't it?" I grinned.

Elton looked at me but didn't answer.

I glanced back at the girl and then at him. "Her name is Hannah? You're sure?"

"Uh, yeah." He swallowed. "Pretty sure. You want me to ask for you?"

"Oh, Elton! Would you?" I smiled my prettiest smile at him.

"Harrumph!"

My head jerked toward the front of the class. Ms. Ingle was really glaring this time. I smiled. She wasn't affected. "Emmalee Bradford, is there something you would like to share with us?"

Everyone stared at me. "Uh—no, Ms. Ingle. Thank you." I smiled really big then. I mean, when the whole class is watching, you might as well look good.

Ms. Ingle rolled her eyes. "Fine. But please try to refrain from speaking out of turn while in my class, okay?"

"Yes, Ms. Ingle, I will try," I promised and then smiled again, just in case.

"Good," she said before turning back to the board.

"I'll have Hannah waiting to be introduced to you as soon as class is over. Just meet us in the hall," Elton mumbled hastily. Then he put his nose in his book and ignored me completely.

When class ended, I put my book and accessories in my Juicy Couture handbag and walked out of the room. True to his word, Elton was waiting for me in the hallway with Hannah.

"Emmalee, this is Hannah Smith," he announced. "I, uh . . . thought you two would, uh, like to get to know one another." He grinned nervously and then hurried off.

She brought her head up from contemplating her colorful bag, and I noticed I was about four inches taller than her. "Hello, Hannah." I smiled my Bradford smile for the fifth time that day.

She said a faint hello and walked away.

Huh? I quickly caught up. "Do you have lunch this hour?"

She turned, clearly surprised. "It's okay, Emmalee, you don't have to do this."

"Do what?"

Hannah stopped so abruptly a guy almost crashed into her. "Get to know me. Just because Elton introduced us, doesn't mean you have to try to be nice, okay?"

Whoa! "What?"

"Really, I won't even blame you if you want to go and find one of your friends. Look, I'll see ya around." She started to walk again.

It took a whole three seconds before I could move. And when I did, I had to practically run to catch up to her. "Wait. Hannah, wait!"

"Yeah?"

"I asked Elton to introduce us. Honestly. If you have lunch right now, do you wanna grab a bite together?"

She switched her bag to her other shoulder. "Why?"

"So I can get to know you."

"Is this some sort of prank or something?"

Flabbergasted, I smiled. I couldn't think of anything else to do. "No. It's not."

Hannah searched my face for a moment and then shrugged. "This better not be, or you'll live to regret it. I've got to drop off a few things first. Where do you want me to meet you?"

"Oh, uh . . . at my car? Do you know which one it is?"

"Sure. Give me about five minutes, okay?"

"All right." My smile stayed in place until she was out of sight. Then I made my way out of the hall into the bright sunshine. *Why doesn't she think I'd want to talk to her? Does she think I'm a snob or something? If so, who else does?* The questions were too disturbing to ponder at the moment, so I shook them off completely as I approached my car.

At the fast-food restaurant, Hannah and I both ordered chicken sandwiches and then laughed at ourselves. It was the first of a surprising number of things we had in common.

"I can't believe you've heard of the band Take That," Hannah declared after sipping on her lemonade. "I thought I was the only person around here who collected their music."

"Are you kidding? I've got every CD they've ever made." I smiled and popped a fry into my mouth. Still chewing and therefore ignoring every rule I'd been taught, I asked, "Okay, so music is a score. How about books? Do you like to read?"

"Do I?" Hannah laughed. "The Hunger Games series is one of my all-time favorites."

"Oh, I've seen the movie, but I haven't read the books yet."

"You have to read the books. They're so intense." She took a bite of her sandwich and then said, "All right. I've got one for you." She leaned forward and raised one eyebrow. "Jacob or Edward?"

Ooh, we are raising the stakes now, aren't we? I decided to play dumb. "You mean in the Twilight series?"

"Of course! What other Edward and Jacob are there?"

"Fine. You have a point." If there was an Edward and a Jacob other than in Stephenie Meyer's romantic thriller series, I had never heard of them.

"You have read the Twilight series, haven't you?" Hannah sounded concerned.

"Uh, duh! What girl hasn't? I totally own them all."

"Me too!" she gushed. "Hardbound and paperback. The paperback are so much easier to carry."

Wow, I like this girl! "No way! I have both sets too, though I'm usually embarrassed to tell people that."

"Sooo, Edward or Jacob?" Hannah asked again.

"Edward. Big shocker there, but definitely Edward."

"Aww, you're kidding! I so heart Jacob."

"Wait, you actually like Jacob?"

"Yeah. He's hot. But seriously, Bella was so not for him—she was way too whiny. Who knew he would end up with—"

"I know! I was that shocked, totally blindsided. You have no idea."

From then on, the rest of lunch was nonstop Twilight talk. I couldn't believe how much fun it was to hash out and debate our differences over the series we both loved. None of my other friends had really gotten into Twilight as much as I had, and it was so cool to finally meet someone who had.

As we pulled back into the school parking lot, Hannah shook her head. "I have to say, Emma, I wasn't expecting us to get along at all. Honestly, you don't seem like the type of person to like all of the cool things you do."

I burst out laughing as I set the emergency brake and turned off the car. "What in the world is that supposed to mean?"

She chuckled, collecting her bag and pushing open the door. "Well, you know—I just didn't expect you to be so easygoing. You're really not what you look like at all."

We climbed out of the car. "Um, thanks . . . I think." I grinned over the hood at her, not sure what else to say.

"It was a compliment, trust me . . ." Hannah's voice trailed off as a group of guys from our football team came up to us.

"Hey, Emma! How come you never return my calls?"

I rolled my eyes at Justin Browning. It was the same question he asked me every day. "You know I don't date high school guys." I moved my purse strap higher on my shoulder and flashed my Bradford smile before walking over to Hannah. I pulled her up over the median to the grass lawn and away from the guys.

"Justin Browning has been calling you, and you don't return his calls?" she said.

"Yeah, long story. Which reminds me, where's your cell? Here's mine. Copy your digits in it so we can hang."

"Sure." She passed me her phone.

Our fingers moved at warp speed. *The mark of true texters.* We grinned as we handed our phones back at the same time.

The bell rang.

"Hey, I'll text you after school, okay?" I said.

"Cool. Bye!" Hannah waved and made her way to the science building, on the opposite side of campus from my next class—art.

I had just finished my English homework when my mom poked her head into the room. "Hey, Emma, you've got a visitor downstairs."

"A visitor?" My brow furrowed. "Who is it?"

"You'll see."

Curious, I stood up to follow her.

"Oh, you may want to change your shoes," she said.

"My shoes?" I glanced down at my glittery flats. "What's wrong with them?"

"Nothing. Except if I were you, I'd wear your Converse or your tennis shoes."

Okay, now I was dying to know what was going on. "Mom?"

"They're in the great room. Hurry, okay?" With a little wiggle of her eyebrows, she was gone.

For Pete's sake. I dug around my closet and found my worn black-and-white-striped Converse. Quickly I slipped my flats off and them on. If there was one thing that drove me nuts, it was surprises—especially surprises where everyone else already knew what the surprise was. I bounded down the stairs and spun on the post as I turned in the direction of the great room. When I crossed the threshold, I stopped, gasping. My hand flew to my mouth to stem the burst of laughter.

There stood Chase, all decked out with a knight helmet and plastic sword. He placed his hand over the hilt of his sword and bowed. "Lady Emmalee, I am at your service."

I giggled—I couldn't help it. "What in the—?"

"What? Can't you tell what I'm supposed to be?" He held his arms out dramatically and made a circle.

He is crazy. "You're a knight."

"Yep. See? I'm your knight, Sir Chase!" He smirked and awkwardly lowered the visor on his helmet. It covered his face.

I began to really laugh. "Oh! Well, Sir Chase, can I ask why you're, uh, my knight today?"

He raised the visor. "Yes, milady, you may." He attempted the accent of an English lord, but failed miserably.

I turned when I heard a giggle behind me. There stood Georgia in shorts and a T-shirt. I grinned with her. Chase cleared his throat and brought my attention back to him.

"Lady Georgia and I would like to take you for a ride on our trusty steed."

"Yeah!" In her excitement, Georgia ran up to Chase and took his hand. "Me and Chase have fixed the paddleboat! We want you to come with us. 'Cept, Chase said you'd be too scared if he didn't remind you he was your knight first."

"He did?" I caught the sparkle in his eyes and for a moment my heart sputtered. One lock of dark brown hair had fallen on his brow beneath the cheesy helmet.

"Is it true, Emma? Are you scared of the lake?"

I looked down into Georgia's sweet blue eyes and answered her honestly. "Yes. Very scared."

"You don't go in the lake at all?"

"Not since I was a little girl."

Her smile fell. "Oh, so you won't go with us?"

"I—uh—" I glanced at Chase. He removed the helmet and our eyes locked, his gaze strong and steady. In that moment, I knew he would never let anything happen to me. I took a deep breath and smiled shakily. "Well, I guess it's safe, as long as my knight is there by my side."

FOUR

Do you have a map?
I keep getting lost in your eyes.

"What are you going to do with them?" I asked after Chase set the helmet and sword on the coffee table.

He looked at them and shrugged. "I don't know. I'm sure they'll come in handy again. Who knows, Georgia and I might ask you to come fishing with us next."

"Ha ha."

Georgia bounced up and down. "Yeah, you have to come fishing with us! I'm sooo good! Even Chase says so, huh, Chase?"

"Yep, even I says so." He grinned at me, his eyes sparkling.

Why is it that the Andersons have the most beautiful eyes? It so isn't fair.

"I wanna hold your hand and Chase's, 'kay?" Georgia clasped my hand before I could answer.

"But what if I want to hold Emma's hand too?" Chase grabbed my hand. "See, this won't work." He leaned down and caught Georgia's hand. "We'll all have to walk in a circle to get to the lake." Georgia and I giggled as he tugged our hands and we began to walk in a circle out of the room.

"Chase, we can't do this the whole way!" Georgia said.

"Why not?"

"Cuz you'll have to walk backwards the whole time."

He stopped. "Oh, you're right—that won't work. I don't suppose either of you would want to walk backwards, then?"

"No!" I laughed. "Ladies do not walk backwards."

"All right. Well, I guess we'll have to do it Georgia's way. Sorry, Emma." Chase grinned as he released my hand and broke the circle.

"That's okay. I would rather hold Georgia's hand anyway, huh, Georgia?"

"Come on. Let's go already. We've gotta get to the lake!" Georgia said as she pulled us both toward the back of the house, her short little legs moving as fast as they could. Chase and I chuckled as we followed.

Soon, we were at lake, with life vests on. I tried to control my unease as Georgia coaxed me to climb onto the paddleboat with her.

"Just step down, you'll be fine." She waved her hands in front of her life vest. "Come on. You can do it."

Great. I'm getting encouragement from a six-year-old. Okay, I can do this. Look, it's only like one foot from the dock. See? One step down.

Just as I had convinced myself to take that step, I felt Chase's arm wrap around my waist. With one leap, we both landed in the rocking boat.

Ahh! My heart jolted within my chest as I tried to recover my balance.

"There, wasn't that easier than worrying about it?" Chase's voice near my ear caused me to let out a delayed scream. The boat pitched wildly to the side when he dodged my shriek, and I clung to him. He put his strong arms around me. "Whoa! Okay, calm down. Hang on. I've gotcha."

After a moment, the swaying stopped and I felt secure enough to relax a bit. "Thanks," I mumbled into his shoulder.

"You're okay now?"

I'm such a wimp. "Yes, I think so."

"Okay, here's the deal. We're going to both sit down together. On the count of three, okay?"

No! I clung tighter and nodded yes.

"One. Two. Three."

We sank slowly onto the wide bench. With the solid plastic beneath me, I let go of his shoulders, first one and then the other. I gripped the seat.

"There you go." Chase chuckled. "Now open your eyes."

Huh? I hadn't even known my eyes were closed. I opened them and squinted at the sunlight bouncing off the water. *Seriously, I have got to get a grip.*

I heard a soft giggle and focused my gaze on Georgia, who sat next to me.

"You really are afraid of the water, aren't you?" she asked.

"Not the water. Just the lake."

"But why?"

"Because, sweets" —Chase leaned over me and ruffled her hair— "when Emma was little, her boat had an accident in the water."

"It did?" Georgia's eyes went wide.

"Yeah, I almost drowned." I attempted to laugh, but it sounded more like a croak.

"Wow! Really?"

"Yep. Chase rescued me." I tried not to look at the vast amount of water all around us.

"Chase did? My brother's a hero?"

"Well, yeah, he is." I looked over at him.

All at once he was a flurry of activity as he got the boat ready to set off. "Don't believe it. I'm not a hero, just a knight doing my duty." He untied the rope from the dock and pushed off.

I held on tighter while the boat rocked a bit and glided away from safety. *Why did the Anderson's have to make such a large lake, anyway?*

"Okay, Georgia, you ready?" Chase asked.

She scooted farther down the seat and nodded. "Yep. Let's go." Her little legs began to pump the pedals.

Chase kept pace with her on the other set of pedals, and we moved slowly across the water. After my nervousness settled, I began to enjoy the sensation of the boat skimming beneath me. I had forgotten how much I loved it.

A few minutes later, I got brave enough to ask, "Are you going to need help, Georgia? I feel bad that you're doing all the work."

She looked up at me and smiled. "No way! This is my favorite part. It's fun."

"It's true," Chase said. "She loves this. It's one of the reasons I had to get the boat fixed so quickly. She was pretty impatient." He looked at me. "So, are you okay? You're hangin' in there?"

"Yeah, actually. It's nice. Thanks."

"Would you ever do it again?"

"What, ride in a paddleboat?" I grinned and leaned back in the seat. "As long as my knight is there."

"Girls. You're all so demanding." He chuckled and glanced out across the lake toward a cluster of trees on the other side. "You know, I would believe you, if you'd actually let go of the seat." He turned back and smiled. "As it is, I'm not sure I'll ever be able to get you back out here again."

I rolled my eyes but decided to answer him truthfully. "Okay, so I love it out here, but yeah, I can't imagine coming back any time soon." I looked down at my hands and realized I was clinging to the seat for dear life.

"Why's that?"

Chase's quiet voice caused me to jerk my head up. Concerned blue eyes glittered into mine. "I—uh, well, there's—I mean, first I'll have to see if I have any nightmares."

"Nightmares?" I thought he would laugh at me, but instead he asked, "Are they really bad? Do you still have them?"

I looked down and nodded. "Look, let's not talk about it, okay? That's all I need to think about right now."

He smiled again. "I'll bet. Okay, so let's change the subject." He leaned back and I watched his legs move a moment before he said, "Oh! So how is your hunt for a new best friend going? Any luck?"

Are you kidding? "You didn't think I'd find a friend very fast, did you?"

"Well, no—"

"Of course I found a friend. She's awesome, too. You'd be surprised at how many things we have in common."

"Really?" Chase looked skeptical. "This is the girl you've decided to make popular? I mean, you're talking about the same one?"

"Of course I am. Her name's Hannah Smith. You would really like her. She's normal and funny, you know? Like, she's not hung up on the newest and latest thing. And she has no idea that she's pretty. Like, none at all. I can't wait to show her how to enhance her beauty."

"Wait." Chase sat up. "So you're going to take a nice, normal girl and turn her into your little clone?"

"What does that mean? My little clone?"

"You don't know what this could—"

"Yes, okay, I want to improve her life. Is that some major crime? She's great and people should get to know her."

"I'm not saying—"

"You know what? I know perfectly well what you're saying, and you're wrong, Chase. Dead wrong! What is up with people thinking I'm some shallow snob all of a sudden? I care, really care about things, okay? And this is something that means a lot to me right now. Just because you can't see the good it will do, doesn't mean the potential isn't there. I'm going to give my friend every opportunity she deserves. Sometimes the difference between success and failure is an open door. Well, I'm opening doors for her."

"Whoa, Emma, calm down a bit."

"Calm down? When you're the one accusing me of—"

"I'm not accusing you of anything." He took a deep breath. "I just hope you know what you're doing, okay? I wouldn't want this to get out of hand."

I rolled my eyes again. "Please, Chase. We're talking a friend here, that's all. I'm not redefining her life or something."

"Chase! Are you gonna help or what?"

We both looked over at Georgia.

"Stop bothering Emma and get moving! We've been going in circles now for like two minutes, cuz you're not doing anything."

Chase laughed. "Aye, aye, Captain, I'll get to it right away."

I shook my head and chuckled at yet another of his bad accents. For a guy who'd lived in foreign places, I was surprised he wasn't better at them.

The next day at school, I was happy to see Hannah waiting for me outside our history class.

"Hey, did you get my text last hour?" she asked as I approached.

"No. Hang on." I pulled my phone out of my bag and glanced down. Three messages waited for me. "Sorry, I've learned not to check at all in Health. Talk about being anti-cell—Ms. Stuart is the worst." I quickly flipped through the other two and opened Hannah's.

> Want 2 study history 2nite?
> Mom's gone says I can hang
> w/u

I looked up and smiled. "I thought you'd never ask!"

"Fab! Hey, I can bring my British boy-band collection? If you love Take That, wait till you hear BoyZone, One Direction, and Snow Patrol. They're so awesome," she exclaimed as we walked into class.

"I've definitely heard of One Direction and Snow Patrol, but who in the world is BoyZone?" I dropped my bag on my desk, and Hannah and I moved to let a couple of students past.

"They're totally vintage—like back in the nineties—but you will so love them!"

"Cool—"

"Hey, Emma." Elton plopped his backpack down on his desk

"Hi," I answered as the bell rang.

Hannah hitched her bag up on her shoulder. "I'm gonna get to my seat. See ya for lunch."

"Perfect."

"So, you and Hannah hit it off, huh?"

I looked at Elton as I sat down. "Yeah, thanks. She's really cool."

"Really? I never thought you'd actually like her." Elton stared at Hannah's back.

"Welcome, fourth-period History," Ms. Ingle said loudly. "Please open your books to chapter 5. Remember, there will be a test on chapters 1 through 5 tomorrow. After we finish this chapter, we will spend the rest of the hour in review. Let's begin."

With so much to absorb, it took all of my concentration to stay with the class. Even then, there were a couple of times I had to call on Elton's superior intellect to help me follow along. *Thank goodness he is next me. Who knew world history would be so much harder than last year's American history?*

By the end of class, my brain was fuzzy. I was relieved to see Hannah looked the same. It was nice to know I wasn't the only one who looked like she needed a stiff lemonade.

"Let's go to Sonic for lunch, okay?" Hannah said as she walked up to my desk. "I could really use a fresh lemon-berry slush right now. You know, something cold and sharp to freeze my brain good and snap it out of this zone."

"How do you do that?" I gasped as I placed my book in my bag.

She grinned. "What?"

"Read my mind! Seriously, how was it we didn't get to know each other sooner?"

Hannah laughed. "I don't know. Give me a few more days and I'm sure I'll start wondering how I ever could've lived without 'Emma the Great' before now. But let's let the oddness of our friendship wear off first. I'm still freaking out that we're even getting along."

I blinked. *Okay, she's smiling, so I'm gonna take that as a compliment.* "Meet you at the car?"

"Sure, give me five again."

As I slowly walked toward the parking lot, I tried not to let Hannah's comment bother me, but between that, and Chase, and Elton's stunned look, it was quickly becoming apparent that people didn't like how I was acting. And it hit home once again that maybe people really did think I was a snob. *But I'm not. Am I?*

FIVE

♥

I better call 911, cuz you're scorchin'!

"Emma! You really don't have to buy me clothes," Hannah said. "Seriously, I have my own money, remember?"

"Will you stop? Besides, what girl doesn't love new clothes?"

"Um . . ." She paused. "All right, I give. No one that I can think of. All girls love new clothes."

"Exactly." I snickered as I climbed out of my red Mini Cooper, fully decked out with a large British flag decal on the roof and two miniature flags on the side mirrors. It was Friday afternoon—just after school—the perfect time of day to go shopping. "Anyway, think of it as doing me a favor, really."

"A favor? Yeah, right!" Hannah smirked as she shut her door. "How is buying me new clothes doing you a favor?"

"Well, ever since my stepdad stayed home sick from work like six months ago, he's been on a do-gooder kick." I clicked the lock and switched my purse to my other shoulder while I waited for her to come around the car.

"How sick was he?"

"No, it wasn't that. See, he was bored that afternoon, so he was surfing the TV channels and caught this old rerun of *Oprah*. It was an episode all about giving to people. I walked in on him crying like a baby. I've never seen him so emotional before. Anyway, later that night he sat me down and told me he'd come up with a plan for our family to give back."

"A plan? You're kidding, right?"

"No, sometimes I wish I was. So here's the deal. I get $350 a month put in my bank account that I can't touch unless I'm giving something to someone else. Then I have to report and tell about my experience to my parents. Well, ta-da! That's where you come in. I heard on the radio last week how Animas Animal Rescue Shelter had already met their quota for this month, so I've been trying to figure what to do with the money. Now, you've just saved me from a massive headache trying to find a different charitable cause. So please say you'll do it. Please?"

"Okay, wait." Hannah stopped just outside the mall entrance. "I mean, yeah, my parents aren't rich or anything, but we have money enough to live on. I'm not sure I want to be thought of as charitable cause."

Ugh. She's so stubborn. "Look, it's not charity, I promise. I have to spend this money somehow. I mean I *have* to. And I would much rather share it with someone I know, rather than a perfect stranger."

"I don't know—it seems weird."

"Only because you've never heard of something like this before. Okay, how about we make a deal. You let me do this thing for you—which would make me super happy—and then I'll let you choose who we help next month."

"You think your stepdad's gonna buy you using me as a charitable cause?" She had begun to cave.

"It's not charity, and of course he will! He doesn't care how I spend the money, seriously, just as long as it's not on me. It'll be perfect—you'll see!" I opened the door and followed Hannah as she walked in. "I'll just tell him I brightened a friend's day by giving her a makeover."

"You totally mean it, don't you? You really plan on giving me a $350 makeover?"

"Um, yeah, that's why I brought it up." I shook my head and smiled at Hannah's shocked expression. "What's the big deal? Isn't a makeover cool?"

"You know you seriously have the craziest parents ever, right? I mean, literally, they are so rock-star, you have no idea."

"Yeah, they're pretty cool." I shrugged before looking up at the array of cheerfully lit stores all around us. *I so heart mall shopping!* "Well, come on. Let's get going."

She dug in her heels as I pulled on her arm. "Do I have a choice?"

"No! Now, come on."

Hannah and I spent a good three hours devouring our favorite stores. Once she got into it, she was a really good shopper. I couldn't believe how much she was able to—under my fashion guidance—get for that much money. I had never looked at the sales racks before; there was really some uber cute stuff for a fraction of the price. Where I would've walked out of the mall with, like, a pair of shoes, a pair of jeans, a light jacket and a couple of tops, Hannah came out loaded. She had like four pairs of jeans, seven or eight tops, a couple of way pretty skirts, a pair of flats, and stiletto heels. And she even had enough money left to get her hair done at a discount beauty parlor.

At the salon, she went in the bathroom and changed into a pair of dark, skinny jeans with her new, sparkly black flats and a black top with glittery pink lips across the front that read, "WANNA KISS? What's it like to want?"

Needless to say, I walked into the mall with an average girl and left with a major hottie. Which would probably explain why Elton almost passed us by as he was walking into the mall and we were stepping out into the bright sunshine.

"Elton?"

"Oh! Hey, Emmalee! What are you doing here?"

"Hannah and I were just shopping. You know, girl stuff."

"Hannah?" Elton turned toward her and his eyes nearly bugged out. "Uh, wow! Um, you—you look different."

I grinned slyly. "Do you think so?"

"Hey, would, um, you two like to go get some Coldstone ice cream or something?" he asked.

Do you think I'm crazy? Like I would pass up Coldstone. "Um, yeah!"

Hannah looked like she was about to faint. "Really? You want to treat Emma and me to Coldstone?"

"Sure. Why not?" Elton laughed. "I like hanging out with pretty girls just as much as the next guy."

Hannah blushed, and I was surprised to see her giggle when Elton stared right at her.

Oh my gosh, why didn't I think of it before? It's perfect. Elton and Hannah. Hannah and Elton. Yes! They are sooo perfect for each other.

Later that night, Hannah and I were in my bedroom chatting about the crazy day.

"Can you believe how sweet he is?" She sounded shocked.

"Well, yeah. He's Elton. Everybody loves him. He's totally nice."

"Okay, but I mean to *me*. I can't get over the fact that the guy even spoke to me, let alone wanted to be seen with me.

I mean, the only guy who ever really notices me is Martin Roberts."

Who? "Come on. You're so gorgeous, seriously. Elton's a guy, and he saw that. Why wouldn't he want to hang out with you?"

"Why? Um, because I'm not his normal type of person to hang with, that's why."

I rolled my eyes. "Puh-lease! Elton is so above that. He's senior class president, for Pete's sake. He represents all seniors, whether they're cool, normal, or not. He would never look down his nose at someone. Really, he is the nicest guy—ask anyone."

"Well, I'm starting to believe it. He seemed really normal today."

I leaned over and grabbed my bottle of silver nail polish off the dresser and started to shake it. Silently, I watched Hannah brush her hair and pull it up out of her face with an elastic band. I decided it was now or never to begin my campaign. "So, did you see the way he was looking at you?" Nonchalantly I unscrewed the lid and began to apply the first coat of polish to my toes.

"Who?"

"Elton, silly."

"Oh. Yeah. What of it?"

I glanced up and raised my eyebrows at her before bringing my other foot forward. "He, uh, was definitely giving you 'the look.'"

She laughed. "Oh, whatever. He was not."

Want to make a bet? "Would you like to do your nails too? I've got more colors in that drawer to choose from." I pointed to the narrow drawer on my white vanity table.

"Sure. Thanks."

"You know, I've seen Elton look at a whole lot of girls, and I've never seen him look at any of them like he did you today," I said as I polished my big toe.

"No way. Are you serious?"

I lifted my head. Hannah held two bottles of nail polish in her hand and was staring at me.

"Perfectly." I shrugged casually and then went back to work on my other toes.

Hannah took the bait. "What's different about it? Didn't he look the same at you as he did to me?"

I finished my toes in agonizing silence before I looked up at her—eyebrow raised—while I put the lid on the nail polish. "No. I would know if Elton was looking at me the same way he was looking at you." I leaned over and set the bottle on my dresser again and wiggled my toes. "I'm sort of an expert when it comes to relationships and guys liking girls. Trust me, Elton is totally crushing on you."

"Are you serious?" Hannah looked like I'd slapped her.

"What? You don't like him?"

She blinked and shook her head slightly. "No, it's not that. It's just I can't believe it, that's all."

"What's not to believe? You're pretty and you're nice. Is there something else out there that you need to attract a guy?"

"But—but, me? Are you sure? Elton and *me?* It just doesn't make sense. Don't get me wrong—I would love it if he really liked me. I just can't get my head around it."

"Well, start getting used to the idea. Because I think you and Elton may become a lot closer than you think."

That did it—she giggled. "Really? You think so?"

"Totally."

"Eek! I can't believe it. Elton Bloomfield, crushing on me!"

My Cheshire-cat smile covered my whole face. *Phase One complete. My senior year just got a whole lot more interesting.*

The next morning while Hannah was in the shower, I ran downstairs to grab a bite to eat and begin Phase Two. My cell was plugged into the wall by the house phone. I picked it up and quickly scanned through my texts before I wrote my own.

> **U no how ur always sayin**
> **u want 2 watch me paint?**
> **Gonna b painting @ home @**
> **2 come on ova & watch. –E**

Less than a minute later, I heard the answering beep on my phone and dropped the cereal box to get it. *Wow. That was fast.* Elton's number flashed at me and I had to smother a giggle when I clicked on the text.

> **Wood luv 2. C u then. Thx.**

"Eeeh!"

"What are you so excited about?"

I turned to my stepdad, who had just come upstairs from the gym in our basement. He looked a little concerned.

"No worries, Dad. Elton Bloomfield is coming over later. He's going to watch me paint Hannah's portrait."

My stepdad grinned, just like I knew he would. He loves Elton Bloomfield. And what's more, he loves it when people develop and use their talents.

"So do you have all the painting supplies you need?" he asked over his shoulder while he reached into the fridge.

"Yeah, I still have all that stuff you got me for my birthday, remember?"

"Okay. That's right." He pulled out some fruit. "You let me know if you need anything else."

"Sure, I will." I walked back to the counter where my cereal was and watched my stepdad as he washed the fruit and began to peel and slice it. He had made a fresh fruit smoothie every morning since I'd known him.

"So what time is Elton coming over?" he asked.

I smiled over a spoonful of Wheaties. "Two." I knew the next question without waiting to hear him ask.

"Do you mind if I talk to him a bit before you girls get started?"

"Sure. I promise not to even set up until he gets here so you can gab with him while I get ready."

My stepdad nodded and then tossed the fruit into the blender. I munched on some more cereal while he collected ice from the fridge dispenser and started the blender.

I'll never understand how a guy with so few words can find so much to talk about, especially when it comes to Elton. Poor Elton. I grinned to myself as I walked to the sink and rinsed the bowl out. *How many times has he gotten stuck talking to my stepdad during a party or something?* Thank goodness Elton was so nice about it. Anyone with eyes—except my stepdad, of course—could tell that Elton only talked to him because he felt he had to. Oh well, it was those qualities that made me positive Elton would be perfect for Hannah. I smiled again as I skipped up the stairs. *Now, to tell Hannah about Phase Two. He he he.*

SIX

I know milk does a body good, but wow,
how much have you been drinking?

"Emma, you're really good."

Elton's response to my painting made me laugh. "You're just being nice. I've totally messed up. I don't know what's with me today, but usually I can paint much better."

"Don't say that. Look at it again. It really does look like her." He paused a moment to examine Hannah as she sat across from us, poised with a book on her lap. "See how you captured her face perfectly? Look at the lips and her eyes and nose. They're perfect—just as beautiful as she is."

Hannah glanced up, clearly shocked. I sneaked a wink at her, and she rolled her eyes and looked down at the book again.

The doorbell rang. "Oh, Elton, would you mind getting that?" I asked as I turned and nearly wiped my brush on his shirt.

He jumped back just in time. "Um, sure. Hang on."

"Thanks." I hurried to straighten the mess I'd made around the table. If it was one of my mom's friends, my mom would never forgive me for cluttering the room. Thank goodness it wasn't.

"Chase!" I stood up as he came in the room behind Elton. "I'm so glad you're here. First, this is Elton, my friend from school. He's the senior class president." Elton lifted his chin in acknowledgment. I ran over to Hannah. "And this is Hannah Smith, the friend I was telling you about. Hannah, Elton, meet Chase Anderson, my next-door neighbor." I beamed.

"Hey, thanks for letting me in." Chase nodded in Elton's direction before he walked over to Hannah and me. "So, I came by to say hi and see if you wanted to come over later and visit the puppies. Hannah can come too."

"Sure. I'm painting her now, but when I'm through, maybe?" I looked at her to see if she was up for the visit.

"Really? Can I see the painting? Is this it?" Chase walked over to the canvas and I quickly met him there.

"It's not done. I mean, it's not that great, either. I'm having a rather odd painting day."

Chase held his chin in his hand and really examined the canvas.

"I think it's amazing," declared Elton as he walked up to us. "Personally, I think Emma's the best painter I've ever seen."

"Really? The best painter?" Chase raised an eyebrow. "Hmm." After a moment of contemplative silence he announced, "I don't know. It's okay. I can definitely see that you have talent, Emma—there's no doubt about that. It's just lacking a few things to make it great."

The nerve. "Great? What do you mean?" I placed my hands on my hips.

"Well, her arms are too long, for one."

"What?"

"And the angle of her head is all wrong. She looks like she's trying to lie down—rather awkwardly—instead of read." He put actions to his words, tilting sideways a bit.

"Her head is fine!" I practically bellowed.

"Yeah, I agree with Emma." Elton came to my defense. "I think she captured Hannah's beauty perfectly."

"Yes, so you said." Chase smirked. "You think she's the best painter ever."

Ugh. "Well, it's obvious *you* don't think I am. Is there anything else you wanted to add?"

Chase grinned and looked at the painting again. "Nope. The arms and the head just about cover it. Other than that, it's a very nice attempt at Hannah's portrait. Very good, Emma."

"Thanks." I raised my eyebrow and he laughed.

"You know what?" Elton said. "I think it's so good I'm going to get it framed for you, Emma. That way you can always see how perfect your painting is."

The last thing I wanted was to look at that picture every day, hung on the wall somewhere. "No, don't worry about it. It's a wonderful thought, and thank you for thinking of it, but really, don't worry about it. Hannah and I were just messing around anyway. It's no big deal."

"Are you sure? My aunt owns a framing shop here in town. Hannah looks so beautiful—I think she deserves to be framed."

Chase choked down a laugh. I glared at him. Just because he couldn't appreciate it, didn't mean he had to ruin it for everyone else.

"Well, thank you, Elton." I smiled smugly at Chase. "You are a great guy." *Unlike some other people I know.*

"You know what we should do, Emma, now that we have these two guys here?" exclaimed Hannah as she stepped forward. "We should have them add to our collection we've been working on."

Perfect. "What a great idea!"

"What collection?" asked Elton.

Chase laughed and shook his head. "There is no way I'm going to get roped into one of your crazy schemes, Emma, so you can count me out."

"Well, for your information, Chase, our collection just happens to be a very uneventful and completely entertaining assortment of cheesy pickup lines we have heard over the years."

"What in the—?"

"But I understand perfectly if you are too stuffy for pickup lines. Don't worry—I'm sure we can get all the help we need from Elton." I straightened my paintbrushes on the small table beside the portrait.

"Yes, Elton." Hannah walked over to him. "I'm sure you know some great pickup lines."

"Actually, I'll have to think about it, but yeah, I'm sure I can come up with a few."

"See, I knew you'd be cool enough to have some," I said to Elton as I looked right at Chase.

He seemed completely unaffected as he handed over a paintbrush I'd missed. "So what's this collection for?" Chase asked. "Any reason you're collecting them?"

Hannah smiled. "It's something I've been doing for a while now, just for fun. Last night I brought my notebook with my collection over, and Emma helped me add a whole lot more."

"I can't believe how many different pickup lines there really are," I put in.

Hannah giggled. "Anyway, now we're trying to see how many unique ones we can find. So will you help?"

Chase stared at Hannah for a moment, then said, "I'll see what I can remember. I didn't use a whole lot of lines on girls. That was my little brother's thing, I think. I've always been more into substance than fluff in a relationship, anyway."

I started to laugh. "Fluff? Come on, Chase, lighten up. Seriously. It's just a fun pickup line—something to make a girl think you're cool and get her to notice you. It has nothing to do with a relationship. Good grief."

He grinned and took a step toward me, causing Elton and Hannah to move back. "So, Emma, do pickup lines work on you? When a guy uses one, does he get a date?"

"Uh, well, no. But that's because—"

"So even if a guy wasted his breath saying one, you wouldn't care, right?" Chase took another step forward. "You wouldn't think he's cool or fun, would you?"

Elton laughed nervously. "Well, I'm personally all about fluff. Especially if it'll make a girl laugh."

Chase raised an eyebrow as he focused his gaze on me. "I rest my case," he said quietly. Before I could respond, he announced to everyone, "Well, I'm off. I promised Georgia I would only be gone for a couple minutes. The puppy invitation is still open, if you girls would like to come by later. It was nice meeting you, Hannah. I'll think of some fluff for your book. And uh, Elton, I hope you enjoy yourself. Good luck getting that picture framed. Oh, and nice painting, Emma." Chase's blue eyes mocked me.

Why do I feel like smacking the guy?

Soon, Elton left too. Just before he walked out the front door, he said, "It really is very good, Emma. I wouldn't worry about what Chase says. He obviously hasn't been around much art in his life."

I thought about Chase's travels abroad and all the art museums he'd visited during those trips, but I kept the thought to myself. "Thanks, Elton."

He seemed pleased with himself. "I can't wait to see it framed. I'll be sure to come over as soon you've finished, okay?

Oh, and Hannah, can I have your cell number in case I come up with any good pickup lines?" He pulled his cell from his pocket.

Her eyes flew to mine for an instant before she glanced back at him. "Sure."

Eeeh! He's getting her number. "Actually, it's probably easier if Hannah types it into your phone," I said.

I smiled when Elton walked over to her, and I smothered a snicker when he leaned over her shoulder to watch her type. *Oh my gosh! They are such a cute couple!*

"Thanks. Cool. I'm glad I finally have your number," he said. "It'll make things a whole lot easier." My heart stopped when he took the phone from Hannah, his eyes never leaving hers. He grinned a totally flirtatious grin right at her.

Hannah giggled. "You're welcome."

With a mock salute and a "Bye, girls," Elton was gone.

I couldn't shut the door fast enough to gauge Hannah's reaction. She didn't disappoint. With a girly squeal, she ran right up and hugged me.

"Oh my gosh! Can you believe it? Elton Bloomfield just asked for my phone number. *Mine!"*

I laughed. "And did you totally hear the way he asked for it? Hello? Can we say pickup line?" I mimicked his deeper voice. "'Oh, Hannah, can I have your cell number in case I come up with any pickup lines?'"

Hannah giggled. "I know. I was so thinking we've got to get the notebook and add that one."

"Definitely an original. I don't think many guys use pickup lines as an excuse to pick up girls."

"You were so right, Emma. I can't believe how much he likes me. Did you hear him go off about the painting? It was crazy."

As I watched Hannah twirl around the entranceway, I gave myself a mental pat on the back. Phase Three had begun.

You know, I should seriously think about starting a matchmaking business. Who knows, maybe one day I'll have my own website.

{♥}

"Okay, that's the guy I've been telling you about this whole time."

I tried to follow Hannah's finger as she pointed to the elusive Martin Roberts. This time, I had tagged along with her before lunch, since she'd said this paragon of manliness usually came and spoke to her then. Because she seemed practically gaga over him, I decided it was wise for me to check him out. I mean, we definitely didn't want anything to scare Elton Bloomfield away.

"Where?" I asked. I still didn't see anyone remotely resembling her description of Martin Roberts, Farmington's president of Future Farmers of America.

"Are you kidding me?" she gasped. "You can't see him? That guy right there. Look again. I'm pointing right at him."

"Do you mean—"

"Yikes! He's coming over. He must've seen me pointing. How do I look?"

Ugh. No wonder why I didn't see him straight away. He wears a cowboy hat, for Pete's sake. That is so Coyote Ugly turn-of-the century. I mean, who does that these days?

"Good afternoon, ladies. Hannah."

I wasn't impressed. Okay, yeah, so he had an accent. I mean, who doesn't love a little country twang every now and then? But he certainly wasn't as hot as Hannah had made him out to be. I glanced at her and stopped just short of rolling my eyes.

She was lost—completely. Utterly and hopelessly lost. It looked like cowboy types were her thing.

"Hi, Martin." She giggled at him.

He lowered his eyes a moment before he looked straight at her. "Hey, you're lookin' real nice today, Hannah. Prettier than I've ever seen ya."

Oh dear, he's shy! She'll probably think that's adorable or something.

"Thanks!" She blushed. "It's all Emma's doing, actually. She helped me fix my hair."

Hannah had managed to stay afloat better than I'd thought. At least she wasn't speechless, or anything.

"Emma?" Martin turned his green eyes on me. "Oh?"

I still wasn't impressed. He definitely wasn't worthy of Hannah's notice, not when she practically had Elton drooling over her. My thoughts must've shown on my face, because Martin gave me a funny look and glanced back at Hannah.

"Uh—well, your hair does look nice." He worked a crooked grin. "'Course, I've always thought it was nice." It was obvious he didn't want to look at me again.

Hannah's cheeks went red. "Really? You've always liked my hair?"

This conversation is getting out of hand. She'll be in love with him before Elton's even made a move. "Hannah," I interrupted, "we've got to get to lunch." I smiled dismissively at Martin before I tugged gently on her arm.

For the first time since he showed up, she looked at me. "Oh, are you hungry?"

"Starved."

Martin touched the brim of his hat. "Then I'll leave you ladies. You two have a good day, ya hear?"

Why does he have to have that blasted Southern drawl?

"We will," gushed Hannah. "You too!"

"Yes, ma'am, I'll try." The guy actually had the audacity to wink before he took a step back and walked away.

"Isn't he hot?" Hannah asked as we made our way across the courtyard to the English building.

How to word this without hurting her feelings? "Um, yeah, he's okay."

"Okay?" She turned toward me. "Are you blind?"

"No. He's okay. But honestly, there are a lot of better guys out there. Take Elton, for example . . ."

SEVEN

Are you a magnet?

Because you sure are attracting me over here!

I was a lot less worried about Hannah's fascination with Martin Roberts once Elton's pickup lines started coming in during lunch a couple of days later. It wasn't really the pickup lines—it was more the words that went with the texts that got me so excited.

"Ooh! I just got another one from Elton." Hannah laughed as she fumbled with her phone. She had set it with a personalized chime so she would know when she got a text from him.

"Well, what does this one say?" I asked.

She scanned the text, giggled, and handed the phone over to me.

> I no its lunch couldn't stop
> thinkn of u heres another 1.
>
> Is there an airport nearby or
> is that my heart takin off?

"Eeeh!" I giggled with her. Phase Three was going even better than I'd hoped. *Martin Roberts will be toast after a couple more of these.*

"So what do you think?" Hannah asked me.

"Think? Are you kidding? I'm thinking the same thing I've thought all along."

"And that is?"

"That the senior class president is seriously crushing on you."

"Do you really think so?" She grinned.

I could tell she totally believed it but just wanted to hear me say it again. I didn't disappoint her. "Hmm . . . let's see. 'I couldn't stop thinking of you'? Uh, yeah, obvious sign of affection right there. If a girl ever needed encouragement, this would be it." I gave the phone back to her and smiled when she dreamily sighed. I had to hand it to her—she was taking it better than most girls would have. After all, he was Elton Bloomfield. I was impressed that Hannah didn't faint or something.

Just then her phone chimed again.

"What? Another one from Elton?"

"Yep." She laughed as she read it. "Holy cow. You have to read this one."

I grabbed the phone and scanned the text.

Hey beautiful must b
something in the air just
thought of another 1.

U must b a broom cuz you
have swept me off my feet.

Talk about staking his claim. "Hello? If this isn't Elton hitting on you, I don't know what is."

"I know. He's totally flirting with me, isn't he?"

"Yes. Come on, let's get back to school. Maybe we'll see him."

There was definitely no other explanation. Elton was head over heels. Hannah and I tossed our food wrappers in the trash and ran out the door, giggling like we were in junior high.

After school, as I was heading toward the parking lot, I received my own text from Elton. Surprised, I stopped on the grass and read it.

> Hey, could u give this 2 hannah when ur done readin it? i wanted u 2 c what i came up with i think its perfect.
>
> There u r... Ive been lookin all ova 4 ya the girl of my dreams!

No way. Elton totally wants me to know how he feels about Hannah. "Oh my gosh—this is just too cool." I couldn't wait to share it with her. Quickly, I scanned the crowd exiting the building. After a couple of seconds I saw her.

"Hannah!" I shouted.

She waved and jogged over to me with a massive smile on her face. "Guess what?" she gushed.

I chuckled. Her enthusiasm was contagious. "What?"

"I'm so excited right now, you have no idea. I just got asked out."

"Are you kidding me? No way. That was fast."

"I know." She twirled around, almost hitting a couple of other students with her bag. "Oops. Sorry."

Elton is so awesome. "So when did he ask you? How did he do it?"

"With this!" She beamed and held out a folded piece of paper.

Huh? "Elton asked you out with a note? You're kidding me?" *How junior high is that?*

She laughed. "No, silly!"

"Oh, for a minute there—"

"It wasn't Elton who asked me out. It was Martin."

"What did you say?" I whipped my head around. "Martin Roberts just asked you out?" *This can't be happening.*

"Well, I haven't answered him yet. I just got it."

"Thank goodness," I muttered.

"Why?"

"I—uh," I started, then closed my mouth. "Nothing." Instead of meeting her eyes, I looked out into the parking lot.

Hannah stepped in front of me. "Emma, is there something wrong? You think I should tell him no, don't you?"

Yes. I smiled my Bradford smile. "Hannah, this is your relationship. If you like him more than any other guy you know, go out with him. I mean, he'll be *your* boyfriend, anyway. I'm certainly not going to get involved if you like him that much."

"Oh." She looked a little upset. "You don't think I should tell him no, do you?"

"I'm not going to say anything. This is your deal."

"Em-ma?"

"Come on, I'll drop you off at home if you want." I smiled and hooked my arm through hers. "Then you can have a chance to think about it and decide if he's the most perfect guy for you."

Looking sad, she glanced down at the letter. "I don't need to think about it. I'll tell him no. I mean, it looks like Elton's going to ask me out anyway, right?" She crumbled up the paper and threw it in the trash can ahead of us and started walking.

I looked down into the can as we passed. "Are—are you sure? I mean, do you want to give it more thought?" *Ah, what am I saying?*

She sighed. "No, I'm good. Besides, he's not anywhere close to being as cool as Elton, anyway."

"Yeah, that's true. Oh, I forgot! Now, that you're going to tell Martin no, I guess I can show you this." I handed over my phone. "Read the last text. It's from Elton. You're going to die."

She quickly devoured it and then threw her hands in the air and shrieked. "Wahoo! I knew it!"

I laughed along with her, causing more of a scene than I had in years. But it was fun. "Okay, so where do you want to go to celebrate?" I asked as we climbed into my car. "Pick anywhere, it's my treat. This is definitely a day for celebration."

Hannah wiggled her eyebrows as she fastened her seatbelt. "Imagine, less than a month ago, Elton didn't even know I existed, and now it's so crazy to think that he likes me." She turned toward me as I backed out of the parking spot. "Okay, so, like, no one knows this, but I have had a secret crush on Elton since the sixth grade."

I shook my head. "No way."

"I know. Can you believe I had to wait until my senior year before my little dream came true? Holy rusted metal, Batman— Elton Bloomfield has a crush on me!"

We shrieked again as I pulled out onto the road. We're girls. Seriously, what else are we supposed to do?

{♥}

That evening, I was helping my mom make dinner when the doorbell rang.

"Would you get it, honey? I'm a mess."

"Sure, Mom." I quickly rinsed my hands and jogged to the door. It was Chase. I could barely make out the huge smile on his face over the large bouquet of flowers in his arms. "Hey you! Come on in. What are those for?"

He stepped over the threshold. "A gift from my mom to yours."

"Oh?"

"They're from the garden," he said. "Our house is chock-full of flowers at the moment, and my dad has banned my mom from bringing any more in. So she sent them to your mom."

"Oh, well, come on into the kitchen. Mom's gonna be really excited." I headed toward the back of the house.

Chase followed. "You know, I'm really glad I saw you. I have some news about your friend Hannah."

"Really? What do you know about Hannah?" Intrigued, I stopped near the stairs and turned around.

Chase moved the flowers over a bit so he could see me better. "She's about to get a boyfriend. A nice one, too."

I grinned. "And how would *you* know?"

"He told me."

Elton told him? "When did you see him?"

"Yesterday, while I was checking out the store for my dad. He works there."

The store? I thought Elton worked at the Pinon Hills Golf Course. "Who's the guy you've been talking to?" I asked suspiciously.

"Martin Roberts." Chase grinned while I stifled a groan. "You know, I've only been here—what two, three weeks? And I have to say that guy impresses me more each time I see him. I really think he's one of Dad's best employees. Anyway, so when I asked if he had a girlfriend—you know, just teasin' him—he mentioned liking Hannah Smith. *Your* Hannah Smith."

"Gee, you don't say."

"Crazy, huh? I told him I thought she was great and that he definitely wouldn't find a nicer or friendlier girl in Farmington."

"Wow. You said that?"

Chase smiled. "Sure. So, it took about ten minutes, but I convinced him to ask her out."

Good grief. "Ugh." I took the flowers from Chase and headed into the kitchen, not caring now if he followed me.

He did. "Emma? What did you mean by that?"

"By what?" I kept walking.

"By that grunt just now."

"Grunt?" I marched over to the countertop and deposited the flowers. "These are for you Mom, from Mrs. Anderson," I explained. "Chase just brought them over. Their garden is bursting again."

My mom looked up from her dough-covered hands and smiled past me. "Oh, thank you, Chase. Tell Grace thanks, and that I said she was very thoughtful."

"I will," he said right behind me as he casually took hold of my elbow. "Just wanted to drop those off. If you'll excuse me, I've gotta run." He turned on his heel and began to bring me with him.

"Okay, bye," my mom called as he maneuvered me out of the kitchen and into the hallway.

"Will you knock it off?" I hissed. I jerked my elbow, but it wouldn't budge from his grasp. We were walking much faster than necessary and Chase Anderson was seriously beginning to get on my nerves.

"Not until you tell me what that grunt meant." He literally propelled me into our front room before he released my arm. "Now talk," he demanded as he shut the door.

"Of all the stupidest, rudest, Viking-est things ever!" I walked right up to him with my hands on my hips.

"Viking-est?" Chase grinned and one eyebrow rose.

I felt like smacking that grin right off his face. "Yes. Viking-est. What are you, some Neanderthal caveman? You can't go around dragging people like that. This is the twenty-first century, and we've evolved since then. I swear, Chase, if you—"

"Emmalee Bradford—" he folded his arms across his chest "—you can rant and rave all you want, but you're not leaving this room until I get some answers."

"You wouldn't dare." I stomped my foot.

His eyebrow rose higher. "Wanna make a bet?"

This is ridiculous. I decided to take control of the situation and let Chase come to me. "Fine," I huffed, then turned around and plopped down on a sofa.

It worked. He walked over and sat on the couch across from me, drilling me with a stare. "So, what do you have against Martin Roberts?"

"Nothing." *As long as he stays away from Hannah.*

"Em-ma?"

He sounds like my stepdad. Irritated, I crossed one leg over the other and willed my foot not to bounce. "Look, I don't have anything against the guy, okay?"

"So why are you acting weird?" Chase asked.

"Because, believe it or not, sometimes you bug me."

"Do I bug you because I talked to Martin? Or do I bug you because I act like a Viking?"

"Ugh!" I leaned forward with my elbows on my knees and put my hands over my face.

"There's that grunt again."

I chuckled and shook my head. "Chase, you really know how to push a girl," I said, my voice muffled by my hands.

He smiled. "I hope so."

I sighed and sat up. "Okay, you want me to be straight with you? Fine. Hannah did get asked out by Martin today, all right?"

"Really?"

"Yes. And no thanks to you, she rejected him."

"What? Why?" Chase looked shocked.

I put my hands on my knees and stood up. He quickly copied me. We had a small, ornate coffee table between us. "You really shouldn't try to set people up. You're not that good at it, believe me. Hannah happens to like someone else—that's why she said no." I put one hand up. "And before you ask if I'm sure, yes, I am. I saw the email she wrote to him."

Chase frowned. "Emma."

Uh-oh, he's upset. "What?"

"You wrote it, didn't you? That email. You were there. You wrote it."

"I—I . . ."

"You know what? I don't care. You—you go and do whatever juvenile high school thing it is you want to do. But you better watch out and be aware of the pitfalls that come from messing with people's lives."

"Whatever!" I said. "What about you?"

"Emmalee, you may think you know it all now, but you don't. You can't—you're just—" All at once Chase stopped, his gaze silently tracing my angry features. He closed his eyes and took a big breath. When he opened his eyes again, they were a deep, sad gray. "I'm sorry to hear that Hannah told Martin no." Chase looked down and shook his head before bringing his eyes back to mine. "I hope he'll be okay."

Frozen in place by the intensity of his gaze, I said quietly, "So do I."

Chase grinned and brought his hands down to catch my fingers. "I have something to say, and I don't want you to take it the wrong way." He squeezed my hands.

What?

"I don't know for certain, but I'm pretty sure you're thinking Elton and Hannah are going to hit it off. Well, if that's the case, I don't want you to get your hopes up. The Bloomfields are known for being, uh, selective when it comes to girlfriends. Believe me, I grew up with Elton's older brother, and it wasn't pretty."

Just when I'd thought Chase was acting decent for a moment, he had to go and blow it. I pulled my hands away from him and folded my arms. "If I was thinking of Hannah and Elton getting together, I would be worried, but since I'm not, I—"

Chase leaned over and kissed me on the cheek, surprising me into silence. "Goodbye, Em."

"You—you're going home?"

"Yeah, I don't want to argue with you." He smiled ruefully. "See ya." And with that he was gone.

EIGHT

♥

I must be a snowflake, cuz I've fallen for you.

After Chase left, I vowed not to feel guilty or get emotional. But I wondered why I felt like crying. *I mean, I was in the right, wasn't I?* I climbed the stairs to my room, debating that question. Martin Roberts didn't deserve my friend Hannah. Besides, it was obvious Elton liked her, and I didn't care who disagreed.

A couple of days later, I hit on the perfect opportunity to show Chase that I was right. I was going to throw a party. A party designed especially for getting a guy to come clean and announce that he loved a certain girl. So when seven o'clock came and Hannah showed up for our study session, I practically dragged her to the upstairs parlor. Mom was reading one of her Regency novels when we burst in.

"Mom, Hannah and I have just come up with the best idea ever!" I could barely contain my enthusiasm. Hannah looked just as shocked as my mom did, but she didn't say anything.

"What is it?" Mom placed her bookmark inside the book and set it on the table next to my favorite chair.

I opted to sit on the small ivory sofa. Hannah hesitantly sat next to me. "I think we should throw a party," I said.

"A party? What kind of a party?" Mom asked.

"I don't know. Something small—I mean, no more than like ten people. I thought we could watch a movie or something."

I glanced at Hannah. She was smiling, and I grinned back.

"Hmm? Are you talking dinner and everything?" my mom asked.

"Well, maybe pizza and popcorn, that kind of thing. Nothing major, Mom, I promise."

"Well, we can't go overboard, you know. Dad can only handle one major party a year. He doesn't like these sort of things."

"I know. But come on, this isn't like your ball or something." My mom's definition of overboard was the Christmas ball she held every year. I did mention she was an Austenite, right? "It's just a few people, honest." I leaned forward. "Look, we can all go to the basement with that big TV and I'll put the movie on down there. That way, you won't even know we're there."

Mom still didn't seem convinced. "Who are you thinking about inviting?"

"Well, Hannah, of course," I said.

Mom smiled at her.

"Elton—Dad likes Elton," I went on. "Um, I was thinking a couple of people from school—"

"How about Chase? Will you invite him?"

"Yes, definitely."

"Good. Now what about the Hart sisters? They could really use a night out—"

"Are you kidding? You want me to invite Cassidy Hart and her little sister?" I frowned. "This is supposed to be a party—you know, where you have fun."

"Emmalee Elaine, they are nice girls. And now that the Andersons are practically related to them, they must be included. What would they think if you didn't invite them?"

"But Cassidy?" Cassidy Hart was one of the few people who truly annoyed me. I couldn't put my finger on why, but that girl really knew how to bug. And her sister! Her little sister was ten times worse. *Ugh.* Just the thought of inviting the Hart sisters over made me not want to have a party at all.

"You know, Emma, I don't know what you have against that girl," Mom said, "but you need to get over it. If you want to have a party, I insist you invite her."

Great. Now I have to throw a party or Mom'll really have a fit. "Fine. Whatever. So can I have one?"

"Sure." She put her hand up. "But don't tell anyone until I talk to Dad. I want him to think this was his idea."

"Okay, I promise I won't." I stood up and Hannah joined me. "Thanks, Mom. We're going to be in my room if you need us."

"Okay."

Hannah waited until we were in my room before she started giving me the third degree. "What was that all about? Why don't you like Cassidy Hart?"

I plunked down on my bed and sighed. "I don't know." I watched as Hannah sank into my beanbag chair. "I wish I did, but I can't figure it out. I mean, she seems nice enough, I guess." I shrugged. "Haven't you ever just met someone you didn't like, for no reason?"

Hannah was quiet for a moment, then smiled mischievously. "Yes, there was someone."

I grinned. "Who?"

She laughed. "You."

"Me? You're kidding, right?"

"Nope. Well, I felt that way until I got to know you. Once I did, I really liked you."

"Seriously? I bugged you?"

"Yeah, but now you don't," Hannah said. "Maybe once you get to know Cassidy, you'll see that she's cool."

"Hmm, maybe." *I seriously doubt it.*

"I've never met her sister, though. What's she like?"

"Claire? You don't want to know," I grumbled.

"No, really. I've heard other people talk about her. Is she all that bad?"

I sat up. "Okay, first off, picture someone who doesn't stop talking—like ever. I mean, honestly, you can't get a word in edgewise. I'm not kidding at all. You just have to listen to what she thinks all of the time. Believe me, it gets annoying really fast."

"So why invite her? Isn't she way younger anyway?"

"Because Cassidy can't go anywhere without her. Do you remember a couple of years ago—it was on the news and everything—about this guy who had been to prison for violating some girl in Colorado? And then he came to Farmington and tried to do it again with another girl? Do you remember that?"

"Yeah, vaguely."

"Cassidy Hart was that girl."

"No way!" gasped Hannah.

"Yep. Taylor and his girlfriend, Chloe—Cassidy and Claire's older sister—caught the guy just in time. Ever since, their parents have freaked out."

"Can you blame them?"

"Well, it's like she's on house arrest or something. Her parents won't let her go anywhere—not even on dates—without her little sister. Claire's like her bodyguard, or chaperone, or something."

Hannah chuckled. "Talk about freak-a-zoid. The poor girl."

"See? And that's what this whole city says about Cassidy, too. 'That poor girl.' It's enough to get on my nerves." I plopped down on my tummy and put my hands under my chin. "Thanks to Taylor, that family totally made instant stardom. And it's all I ever hear about—Cassidy Hart this, and Cassidy Hart that. Believe me, if you had to live with that name ringing around your head as much as I have, she'd drive you nuts, too."

Hannah laughed and kicked her shoes off. "I don't doubt it. I can see what you mean now." She fluffed the beanbag behind her and rested her head, still facing me. "So what's she like at parties?"

I sighed. "Well, before the—uh, incident—she was okay. I mean, kind of outgoing and stuff. But I think it messed her up. Or maybe just being around her sister so much stopped her from talking, because she hardly does now. She's almost kind of—I don't know . . . shy. It annoys me that she has become this sort of mousy person that everyone fawns over. Like, get over yourself and get on with it already."

Hannah giggled. "I'm so glad you're inviting Cassidy."

"You would be!" I chucked a pillow at her and missed.

"I can't wait to see how you'll react when she's around." Hannah chucked the pillow back. It flew over my head and bounced off the headboard.

"Aha! See, that's where you'll be sorry. I'll be perfectly nice. No one will know that she isn't my best friend." I threw the pillow back and it landed with a *wham* on Hannah's shoulder.

"That's it!" She grabbed the pillow and stood up.

I shrieked and jumped to reach for another pillow, but it was too late. Hannah's pillow crashed into my back, the force tipping me forward. "Ahh!" I snatched the pillow up and collected the other one before turning around. Hannah held the huge beanbag chair over her head, ready to defend herself. Laughing, I collapsed on the bed.

She snickered and raced forward. I screamed and tried to block the blow of the beanbag with my legs. It worked until my sock got caught on the zipper. And then *rip!* Millions of little Styrofoam balls flew around the room, creating the best faux snow scene ever.

The day of the party was perfect. Perfect day, perfect weather, perfect time. I even had the perfect movie to watch—*Hitch*. It was several years old, but still so funny and a great party mixer. The pizza had arrived, the buttery popcorn had been popped, and snacks and candy filled small bowls throughout the TV room in the basement. Large, multicolored pillows were scattered on the floor and couches. There was even an assortment of beverages chilling in the fridge in our small basement kitchen.

It was destined to be an awesome night, filled with all sorts of romantic possibilities. I had a feeling Elton wouldn't be able to resist and would come clean tonight. In fact, I was sure Hannah was going to have a boyfriend by the time she went home.

And what better setting for it than a movie? It's the perfect time, when the lights are low, to hold hands and sit a little closer.

I couldn't wait to see Hannah and Elton hold hands. During a stroke of genius, I called Elton and asked him to stop by and pick her up for me. He was more than happy to oblige. I couldn't wait for her to tell me all about riding in his car. *Eeeh! I am so good at this matchmaking thing.*

I took one final glance around the cozy room and willed myself not to actually squeal out loud. The doorbell rang. When

I opened the front door wide, I was surprised to see only Elton. I looked past him down the walkway, but no one else was coming up. "Hannah? Is she—?"

"Oh, she didn't tell you? I thought you knew."

A sinking feeling hit my stomach. "Knew what?"

"She can't make the party."

"What?!" My mouth dropped open. "Hannah can't make the party? What do you mean? Why? Did—"

"She's sick." He sighed.

Oh no. "You're kidding! What does she have?"

He looked so bummed I almost kissed him. "Her mom thought it was food poisoning, but she wasn't sure."

"No way. Food poisoning? That's terrible." The poor girl was probably puking her guts out.

Elton sighed again and rubbed his foot against the step. "Yeah, I feel awful for her—you have no idea. I mean, I was really looking forward to hangin' with her."

"Really?" I tried to hide my smile.

"Yeah." He sighed again and then shrugged his shoulders. I was impressed by the way he was able to control his disappointment until he said, "Oh well. At least *we* aren't sick. I mean, it's one thing for Hannah to miss a party, but for me and you that would be the worst. I hate missing parties. Besides, it's always better to have one less person than one more, don't you think? It makes it more special if there are just a few people." He smiled as he walked past me into the house. "Yum. Do I smell pizza? I love pizza."

Baffled, I closed the door and rushed to catch up with Elton. He was following his nose down to my basement. *Good grief.* "Yeah, um, the pizza is down there," I called down the steps. "Help yourself."

"Thanks. I will."

The doorbell rang again and I tried to brush off his almost rude behavior as I retraced my steps. *Maybe he's just more disappointed about Hannah than he's letting on.*

When I swung the door open wide, Cassidy and Claire Hart stood on the porch.

"Hi!" I said as happily as I could. "You made it." *Darn it.*

Cassidy opened her mouth to speak, but her younger sister beat her to it.

"Wow!" Claire gasped as she stepped in the house. "I forget how cool this place is! It is really one of the prettiest homes I have ever seen—don't you think so, Cass? I bet Chloe would love it here. Has she ever been here? Oh, I smell pizza! Did you cook it? Or did you order out? What pretty flowers! These look just like the flowers in our front yard. Don't these look just like the flowers in our front yard, Cass? Cassidy loves flowers, don't you? And what a pretty table! Is it an antique? Our mom loves antiques, but we can never afford them. Oh! Before I forget, Chase said he was parking the car at his house and would be over in a minute—"

"Wait!" I had to interrupt. "Chase? Did he drive you or something?" I looked over at Cassidy, hoping she would answer.

"Yes, he did." Cassidy blushed and looked down.

"It was the nicest thing ever!" Claire rushed over to my side. "He has the most beautiful car in the world. Cassidy was saying how beautiful it was, weren't you? We never thought anything would be more exciting than Taylor's car. Chase is so nice. And his car is so comfortable—"

I was saved from having to hear more when the guy in question showed up. "Speak of the devil!" I smiled frantically at him while I closed the door that had been open this whole time. "I'm so glad you're here."

"I bet you are." He looked past me and smiled at Cass and Claire.

"I'm still waiting for a few more people," I said. "Hannah's sick, so she isn't going to be able to make it. Could you host for me for a few minutes?"

"Sure. It's downstairs, right?"

"Yep." I gave Chase my prettiest smile.

He smiled back, but whispered as he walked past, "All right, but you owe me."

"Chase! Are you going to go down with us too?" Claire was off again. "You are so nice—"

Ugh. So much for thinking this party was going to be amazing. I think I have a headache.

NINE

Are you from another planet?
Because there's nothing else like you on earth!

The last of the guests were leaving. The movie was over, but no one had really been able to watch it, thanks to Claire's nonstop commentary. *That girl drives me nuts.*

I did try to talk to Cassidy before we started the movie, but the only words I could get out of her were "yes," "no," and "thank you." Talk about a walking zombie. It was so annoying. The worst part was I seemed to be the only one completely miffed by the situation.

There was one good thing that came out of the party, and one good thing only. Carson and Madison—two guests who had come in a little later than everyone else—announced that Carson's younger brother Ethan was coming home from New Mexico State University for Thanksgiving week. Since Thanksgiving was less than a month away, I found that very promising.

Ethan Franklin was one guy I had always wanted to get to know. He had graduated a couple of years earlier, and even though I could vaguely remember him, I'd never really talked to him. The funny thing was, everyone I knew who knew him said he and I would be the perfect couple. I, of course, took that as a major compliment, since the guy was known to be pretty cool, not to mention somewhat of a celebrity, since he was Farmington's reigning four-wheeling champion.

Still, the news that Ethan Franklin was coming dimmed in comparison to what a disaster the party had been. Even Chase, probably bored out of his mind, left early due to a cell-phone call that saved him from answering another question from Claire.

I picked up a pillow and tossed it on the couch. Elton was gathering the candy bowls from around the room.

"Thanks for staying and helping." I smiled up at him.

"Hey, no problem. I figured you'd want me to stay anyway."

"Um, yeah." *Maybe he wants to talk about Hannah.*

"I'm going to run these bowls upstairs. They go in the kitchen, right?"

I nodded as I reached down and picked up two more pillows. "Just set them in the sink, please. I'll wash them later."

He had already taken the pizza boxes up. I had to say the room cleaned up pretty fast, though it still needed a quick vacuum. I picked up the last pillow and arranged it nicely on the couch, before sinking down with a sigh. I closed my eyes and allowed myself to relax. *What a wasted evening.*

A couple of seconds later, I felt the cushion beside me give way as Elton sat next to me. I could tell it was him by the way his cologne attacked my senses. *Ugh! How close is the guy, anyway?* I opened my eyes and nearly jumped. His face was just above mine.

"Hello, beautiful," he whispered. "Is it hot in here, or is it just you?"

"Are you kidding me?" I gasped and backed away.

Elton followed. "I know you've had a thing for me for a while now."

"Excuse me?" My back hit up against armrest.

"It's okay. You don't have worry anymore, cuz I like you too."

Oh no, oh no, oh no! This can't be happening! I sat up, forcing him to move back. "Elton! Hello? I'm Emmalee Bradford, remember?"

"Oh, I remember." One long arm slid behind me on the couch. Before I could even shriek a protest, I was on Elton's lap. I didn't even know he was that strong. He definitely didn't look that strong. "How could I ever forget you?" he whispered in my ear. His other arm slithered around my waist, capturing me neatly within his grasp.

"Elton, are you drunk?" I pushed against his chest, trying to free myself.

"Drunk?" He chuckled at my attempt to escape.

Does he think this is cute or something? I swear I will kill the guy if he tries anything. I don't even care how much Hannah will miss him. There is only so much a girl can put up with. "Elton, I'm not Hannah. Save your breath for her."

"Hannah?" He laughed derisively. "Who wants to think of Hannah when Emma's on his lap? Mmm, this is better than Christmas. Come on, baby, give me a kiss. I've been waiting all night to taste those juicy lips." He pulled me even closer.

All right, that's it. Elton Bloomfield has seriously just messed with the wrong girl. I pulled my left arm back as far as I could and punched him in the eye.

"Ahhh . . . Ow!" Instantly, I was shoved ungraciously off his lap and landed with a thud on the imported Turkish rug. Before I could get to my feet, Elton was pacing the room with his hand covering his eye. As I stood, he turned and flung a whole slew of profanity right at me.

Good. I'm glad he's mad. Pain shot through my hand. I knew it would be bruised, but it was nothing compared to what Elton would see in the mirror in the morning. He was lucky he'd only experienced my left hook. My right one was way better, but that hand had been preoccupied keeping me off the loser. I smiled so he could see I wasn't affected by his boorish manners. I walked over to the stairs.

He moved closer. "Why'd ya do that, huh?" he spat at me while he glared with his one good eye.

With about two feet between us, I clenched my right fist, ready to use it if I had to. When I didn't answer, he lost it.

"Who do you think you are, anyway?" His lone eye pierced me as saliva flew from his mouth. "You think you're some sort of princess?" He nearly choked on the word. "You've been leading me on for weeks now. And then as soon as I start playing your game and give you what you want, you hit me. What is that about? I think you need to be taught a lesson."

Rage filled his eyes as he menacingly raised his arm. I gauged the exact moment to counteract his strike and give him the uppercut he deserved. *Forget my hand. This boy is going down.*

"That's enough," said a deep voice behind me.

Elton startled. It was just the leverage I needed. I locked my fist and aimed it directly for his jaw, right underneath his chin.

"Em, no!"

My right arm was seized and jerked back a whisker's breath away from knocking the loser senseless. *Dang it, Chase!* "Let me go!"

I watched a stunned Elton stumble backwards and away from me.

"You really didn't want to do that," Chase said in my ear.

"Yes, I did!" I tried to free my arm. "I had him. He totally deserved it."

"There's no doubt in my mind that he deserved it. But think about it. You really want to break your hand over the guy? Doesn't the other one hurt enough already?"

"You've gotta ruin everything, don't you?" I sulked, not willing to give in to his superior intellect.

He chuckled and slowly wrapped his arms over mine around my waist and then rested his chin on the top of my head. For a moment I was lost in the feeling of my knight surrounding me. I allowed my head to rest on his chest and relished the deep voice as it vibrated above me.

"Mr. Bloomfield, you've got approximately ten seconds to gather your things and get out of this house, or I won't hold Emma back. And then when she's through with you, I'll really let you have it."

"W–when did you get back? I . . . I thought y–you left the party," sputtered Elton.

"Eight seconds," Chase said calmly.

"But—but—!"

"Seven, six, five . . ."

"All right, I'm going! Give me a second."

"You have three."

"Ahh!" Elton grabbed his keys and bolted past us for the stairs.

"One." Chase laughed as the front door slammed shut and echoed all the way to the basement. "So, are you gonna tell me what that was all about?"

"No!" I pulled out of his arms and turned around so I could see him. "What are you doing here? When did you get back? How come nobody tells me anything around here anymore?"

Chase tried to smother a grin. "Didn't I tell you I'd be back?"

"No, you didn't." I folded my arms.

"Well, aren't you glad I came?" He chuckled at my expression. "Okay, so obviously you're not, but . . ." He sighed and shook his head as he took a step closer. "Look, it's understandable that you wanted to deck the guy—believe me, I wanted a piece of him too—but what am I going to do with you, huh?"

"You don't have to do anything with me. I'm a big girl now. Good grief! You treat me like I'm your little sister."

Chase took another step forward. "Do I? I'm sorry, I don't mean to."

"Y–you should be sorry." I was having a hard time remembering to be mad when he was this close. "I—I already have an older brother."

"Hmm. That's right, you do." He took another step closer and reached out to touch my sleeve. He brought his gaze back to mine. "Well, how about a friend, then?"

"A friend?"

He twirled the soft fabric between his fingers.

"Do you need a friend?"

"Um." I licked my lips. "I was pretty good with the knight thing, really."

Chase laughed and stepped back, releasing his hold on my senses. "Well, in that case, I guess you're happy I rescued you."

"Yeah—no. Ugh." I walked over to the basement closet and pulled out the vacuum. "For your information, everything was fine before you came. And everything would've been fine had you never come at all."

He didn't say anything as he plugged the cord into the electrical outlet. After a few more seconds of silence, I started the vacuum and attacked the rug. Chase waited until I finished, then gently took the machine away from me. He turned it off and asked, "Better?"

"A little."

"So are you gonna be straight with me or what?"

"Or what."

He grinned. "Touché."

I chuckled and shook my head. "What do you want to know?"

He walked over to the wall and unplugged the cord, then headed back to the vacuum and slowly wound the cord into place. "You were hoping Elton would go for Hannah, weren't you?" he said finally.

I watched Chase put the vacuum in the closet and shut the door. Then he turned around and said, "By your silence, I'm assuming yes." He walked back over to me.

"So what if I did want Elton and Hannah to get together—why should it bother you?"

"A lot of reasons. Emma, you really couldn't see that he liked you more than her?" Chase leaned against the back of the couch and crossed his ankles. "Even I could see he liked you more than her, and I was only around you guys once."

I turned away from Chase, absentmindedly running my fingers around the cover of a light switch. I finally I gave up and sighed. "What am I going to do?" With my back to him, I rested my head on the wall and willed myself not to cry. "She's my best friend, no matter what you think about it. She is. She doesn't deserve to have her heart broken like this. It's not fair." I stood up. "Ooh! Elton Bloomfield is such a jerk!" I spun around to face Chase. For a moment I was caught by the unexpected sympathy in his eyes. "I—I—" I blinked and looked away. "I can't believe I, for one minute, thought he deserved Hannah."

Chase cleared his throat. "It's true. Hannah is a much better person than he his. I only wish…" Chase's voice trailed off. To his credit he didn't say "I told you so," but I could tell it took effort.

"H–how is Martin? Have you seen him?"

Chase took a deep breath and stood up. "Yeah, I've seen him. He's not doing so great."

"Really? I hope Hannah didn't hurt him when she told him no."

Chase shook his head and looked down at the floor. "I don't think anyone could be more upset than Martin is. I think he really liked her. It'll take a while to get over it."

"Oh." I felt awful. "I'm sorry."

Chase looked up. "Me too."

"Here." I opened my arms wide. "Hug me, and we'll call a truce, okay?"

He hesitated, then walked into my embrace. His strong arms wrapped around my waist, and I smiled when I felt his nose press into the side of my cheek. *Maybe having another older brother isn't that bad after all.*

TEN

If I followed you home, would you keep me?

The next morning was bleak, especially once the memory of the past night came back in full force. I sat in my bed and contemplated just how I was going to break the news to my sick friend. No girl should ever have to deal with this sort of anxiety first thing in the morning. It really was awful.

After taking a shower I felt better—at least well enough to make the phone call. Dressed and sitting on the stuffed chair in my room, I took a deep breath and punched Hannah's number.

She answered after one ring. "Hello?"

"Hi, Hannah, it's Emma."

"Hi! How did the party go? I'm so sorry I missed it. I felt horrible not going. It's just I kept getting sick and having to run to the bathroom, and I would forget to call you. Please, please, please say you forgive me. I hope you know I definitely wanted to come. I still feel sick or I would've been over to your house already to apologize."

That's ironic. "Yeah, Elton told me. Actually, about El—"

"Oh, good. I'm so glad he told you! It was so embarrassing, too. I'd gotten sick so fast that I didn't have time to call him. I couldn't believe it when he showed up at my door. I was mortified! Thank goodness my mom screened him for me. There was no way I was going to let him see me like that."

"I don't blame you," I said. "I wouldn't want to—"

"So what did he look like?"

"Uh, Elton?"

"Duh! What was he wearing? Did he look totally hot? Did he ask about me? Was he worried or grossed out or something?"

"Grossed out?"

"I mean, was he mad that I hadn't called him first?"

"Oh, uh, no. He didn't seem mad."

Hannah sighed. "That's good. I was so worried."

This is going to be so much harder than I thought. I debated putting it off a couple more days until Hannah felt better, but then quickly scratched that. It was better if she heard it from me first. I was positive Chase wouldn't say anything, but I couldn't guarantee Elton wouldn't. And he had a lot of friends.

I took a deep breath and plunged right in. "Listen, Hannah, I need to tell you something."

She was silent for a moment. "Oh, okay. Is it bad?"

"Actually, yeah. It is bad. And you're not going to be happy with me when I say it."

She chuckled and then groaned into the phone. "Don't make me laugh, it hurts my tummy."

I smiled nervously. "I'll try not to. But seriously, you're not going to like me much once I tell you my news."

Hannah was quiet a moment, then said, "Emma, what is it?"

I took a shaky breath. "Well, it's, uh . . . about, um . . ."

"Egads! Will you just tell me already? You have no idea how tight my hand is holding onto this phone."

I tried again. "It's about El–Elton."

"What about him?" Her voice caused me to grip *my* phone tighter.

"Well, he . . ."

"He what?"

I opened my mouth and then hesitated. I really, really, didn't want to tell her. Why did Elton Bloomfield have to be such a loser? Such an idiotic, brainless loser?

"Emma, is it that bad? Why won't you tell me?"

"Yes, it's that bad. And I—I don't want to tell you because I don't want to hurt you."

"He's in love with someone else, isn't he?"

I gasped at Hannah's intuitiveness. Or maybe she'd heard already.

"I'm right, aren't I? He has girlfriend, doesn't he?"

"No!" I nearly yelled into the phone. "He doesn't have a girlfriend. He can dream, but he won't ever get the girl he wants."

"Emma?" Hannah whispered. "Who is she?"

I clamped a shaky hand over my mouth to muffle the sobs that were desperate to come out. Tears came to my eyes and I blinked rapidly to stop the tears from falling.

"Emma? Who is it? Tell me, please."

A small, heart-wrenching sob escaped my mouth. "It . . . it's me." I lowered the phone and stifled a few more sobs. When I had better control over myself, I brought the phone back up to my mouth. "I—I'm so sorry, Hannah. I'm so sorry. I had no idea. None. If I did, I would've never, ever thought to—I would've never made him think that . . . made you think that . . ."

"Emma, Emma, it's okay."

"I'm sorry."

"Hey, I know you are." Hannah took a deep breath. "Look, I'm sorry you had to be the one to tell me. It's not fair, is it?"

"You're sorry, but—"

"Emma, stop it. Neither of us can change the facts. So he didn't like me, big deal. Okay, so it is a big deal, but I'm gonna get over it. You definitely don't have to cry about it. I mean, honestly, you have to admit it was weird that he started to like me in the first place. Hello? The senior class president falls for, well, uh, me. It doesn't add up."

"Yes, it does!" Now I was getting mad. "Elton Bloomfield is a jerk, seriously. If he can't see you for who you are, I'm glad we got rid of him when we did. The moron."

"But Emma, think about it. Honestly, of course he would have fallen for you. He's probably always been crushing on you. You're Emmalee Bradford, for crying out loud. It was probably like some junior high fantasy come to life when you actually started to include him in stuff. Don't knock Elton just cuz he saw you before he saw me."

"But he was totally flirting with you!"

"Yeah, but to him it might've not meant anything more than getting on your good side by being nice to me." Hannah took an unsteady breath while I absorbed what she said. "Look, I'm gonna go now, okay? I've got a headache and I'm starting to feel a little queasy again."

"Okay."

"But I promise I'm not mad at you, all right?"

I breathed a sigh of relief. "Really? Okay."

"Don't worry about it. I'll get over him eventually."

"You really are an awesome friend," I said brightly. "And we're gonna find you the most perfect guy, I promise!"

She chuckled. "Well, not right now, please. I need a little bit to get over this one first. Then we can begin guy hunting again."

"Hannah?"

"Yeah?"

"Thanks for understanding."

"I'll call you tomorrow, okay?"

"Okay." I hung up the phone, then walked over to my bed and collapsed. All along I'd thought I was helping Hannah. But after experiencing her amazing kindness and friendship, I realized she was really helping me. If every girl had a friend like Hannah, the world would be a brighter place.

"So have you chosen which puppy you want yet?"

I turned at the sound of Chase's voice as he came out of his house onto the porch. Georgia was up off the grass and running to him. "Chase! Chase!" she squealed while a mountain of little fluff balls yapped and chased her.

"Whoa!" He stepped back and picked Georgia up, probably to save the puppies from her eager feet, before carefully walking to my side. The miniature Pomeranians leapt and bounded wildly around his legs. In fact, there was no way he was going to be able to sit down on the grass without smashing one of them. "Uh, I think I'm gonna need some help." His sky blue eyes twinkled down into mine.

I laughed and tried to collect as many of the little guys as I could. Except they were all excited to see Chase, and one would quickly spring out of my lap as soon as I leaned over to grab another one. "The little rascals love you too much. It's impossible!" I giggled as another one escaped and bounced over to Chase again.

"Yeah, Chase," said Georgia near his ear, "them li'l rapskulls keep getting away!"

I finally gave up. I stood and brushed my jeans off, looking for a chair. *There's one.*

"Hey!" Chase called as I jogged over to the porch. "You can't leave me like this!"

I grabbed the lightweight garden chair and brought it over to him. "See, I'm nicer than you thought."

"You're an angel!"

After I placed the chair away from the excited puppies, Chase cautiously made his way over to it and slowly lowered his tall frame.

"Just don't forget, the next time I make you mad, I'm an angel." I grinned as I sat down on the grass near the chair.

"Oh, darn. I said that out loud, didn't I?"

Georgia squirmed off Chase's lap. "Wait till you see the one Emma wants."

We both watched her pursue my favorite puppy. The little dog obviously found the flower garden much more exciting than Chase's shoe, which seemed to mesmerize the other three pups.

"So you picked one, did ya?" he asked.

I looked up at him. His eyes were focused on Georgia. "Yeah, I chose Clementine."

"Clementine?" That got his attention. He looked down at me and smirked. "Who in their right mind names a puppy Clementine?"

"Your mom."

"What? You're kidding! When?"

I giggled. "Just this morning."

"Are you gonna keep the name?"

"I don't know, I might."

Chase shook his head. "Women. You do know that's a cow's name, don't you?"

I threw back my head and laughed. "Chase Anderson, you're horrible."

He grinned and picked up Little Lion, who was trying to scramble up his pant leg. "Come here, you." He brought the puppy right up to his face. "Come save me from silly girls." The puppy excitedly yipped and wiggled his tail. Chase brought the little guy closer and gently rubbed his jaw over its head. "Have you talked to Hannah yet?"

I looked away, watching Georgia laugh and run from a couple of puppies. "Yeah, I called her this morning."

"Good."

I met Chase's gaze briefly before lowering my eyes. I could feel his stare as I examined my colorful shoes.

"How is she?" he asked.

I shrugged and fiddled with some blades of grass. "Not good. Not bad, but not good."

"Did she cry?"

I breathed out a puff of air. "No, but I did."

"You, Emma?" He ran his hand through my hair, making tingles race up and down my spine. "I can't imagine you ever crying over anything. You're one tough girl."

"Am I?"

"Yep. That's what I like about you."

"Except for when I'm near the lake." I laughed quietly.

His fingers drifted through my hair a second time and I tried to cover the shiver. It didn't work.

"Hey, are you cold?" Chase removed his hand.

"No." *Just oversensitized.*

"Are you sure? We can move back inside if you want."

"I'm fine, really." I decided to change the subject. "Hey, while you were gone from the party last night, you missed the news."

"What news? I thought the only exciting thing was Elton's news."

"Oh, please!" I rolled my eyes and looked up at him. "This news is way better than Elton."

"So what's up?"

"Carson Franklin said his little brother Ethan is coming home from NMSU for Thanksgiving."

"Really? And this is exciting why?"

"Um, hello? Ethan Franklin. *The* Ethan Franklin. I've only wanted to be introduced to the guy for two years."

Chase looked over at Georgia. "So, uh, you really like this guy, huh?"

I laughed. "What's not to like? He's supposedly hot. He's nice. He's funny. Everyone says we'd be perfect together. And to top it all off, he's amazing at four-wheeling."

"Really? A four-wheeling buff?" Chase glanced back down at me. "So, you're planning to hang with him?"

I laughed. "I don't know. We'll see. First, I have to see if he likes me."

"Oh, he'll like you."

"Really? You think so?" I knew I was glowing.

Chase nodded, then looked back toward Georgia and muttered, "What's not to like?"

ELEVEN

♥

Hey, is it just me, or are we destined to be married?

The following Monday at school, Elton treated me like I had the plague. When we met in the hall, he refused to look at me and quickly moved to the other side. Which was fine, because I definitely didn't want to be anywhere near him. His black eye must have been downright nasty. He had special permission from his doctor to wear sunglasses all day at school—some random excuse about the ultraviolet lights from the classrooms hurting his eyes. *Yeah, right, he probably bribed the doctor to say that! The dork.*

Okay, so I admit it. I thought Elton's behavior was completely hilarious. That is, until I walked into history class and overheard him mocking Hannah. Even after his actions the night before, I couldn't have imagined him being so harsh. When I realized the rest of the class was egging him on, I was mortified for Hannah. One look at her face and I nearly decked Elton again. But I knew she would kill me if I did, so instead I took a deep breath and pasted on my Bradford smile. Everyone stopped laughing and stared at me. That smile really was killer. *That's right,* I thought. *And don't you forget who really owns this school. If you want to be popular, you better stay on my good side.*

"Oh, there you are, Hannah. I just got your text." It was no trouble at all to walk past my usual seat and sit up front in the empty one next to her. In fact, it felt liberating. After that one small act, no one would dare insult her again. Only somewhat mollified—I would've rather blackened Elton's other eye—I smiled down at my friend, who looked relieved. I knew she would never mention it, and I vowed right then to pretend I had no idea what had just happened.

"I hope you don't mind if I sit here."

"Mind?" She rolled her eyes. "Why haven't you earlier?"

I thought a moment. Oh yes—I had stayed next to Elton to hear all of the flattering remarks he would make about her. I couldn't tell her that. "Uh . . ."

"Miss Bradford, are you and Hannah finished with your discussion?" asked Ms. Ingle. Her arms were folded and she was tapping her high-heeled shoe against the carpet.

"Uh, yeah. Sorry." I smiled.

Ms. Ingle took two strides up to my desk. "So, Emmalee, are you planning on making the front row a permanent spot?"

My smile grew. "Well, yeah, actually. That is, if you don't mind." I could feel the whole classroom staring at the back of my head, so I sat up a little straighter and announced loudly, "Hannah and I have been working together on our reports and stuff. It would make it a lot easier and way more fun if we were together."

"Would it?" Ms. Ingle raised an eyebrow. She glanced toward Hannah and then to the back of the room where Elton was sitting, before looking at the rest of the students. Her eyes sparkled when they came to rest on me again.

She knows what I'm doing!

"Yes, I can see why it would be much more entertaining to be up front here with Hannah." Ms. Ingle glanced around the room again, then gave me a quick grin. "You are more than welcome to stay here."

"Thank you!" I gushed.

She narrowed her eyes as if to warn me not to overdo it.

I smiled. Maybe Ms. Ingle was more human than I thought.

After Monday, Hannah didn't have any problems with Elton, and school basically whizzed by in a blur. There was a brief uncomfortable moment when everyone but me was invited to Cassidy Hart's themed Halloween party. Not that I would've gone had she invited me—I just found it odd that she didn't.

It wasn't even that big of deal when I went with Hannah to find the perfect costume. This year the party had a Mafia theme, and she wanted to find a 1940s-type dress and hat. *Okay, so how lame are Halloween parties, anyway? Especially ones where you dress up. Can we say grade school? Except, that's what I don't get. Why do I care? Why is it totally bugging me that I wasn't invited? I abhor dressing up in costumes.*

"Hey, Emma, you've gotta check out this one!"

I looked across the shabby thrift store where Hannah had insisted we shop in first. She held up a dark purple satiny dress. "Wow. That would work," I said. "It's even got shoulder pads."

"I know. And check out the skirt on the dress. It's perfect!" She brought the dress in front of her and beamed down at it. "Oh, so have you found any costume jewelry that'll work yet?"

"Hmm . . ." I glanced back at the glass-topped case and eyed the sparkly, multicolored faux gems. "There's a few things that could work." And then I saw it. "Wait! There's an awesome— like really cool—purple and turquoise butterfly pin thingy."

"Really? A brooch?" Hannah called back.

"Yeah." I waved my hand, beckoning her over to the case. "Come and look! Seriously, bring the dress, too."

She hurried over and leaned around my arm to get a better view.

"Excuse me," I said to the clerk at the adjoining counter. "Can we see this brooch—the butterfly one?"

"Sure." The clerk smiled and walked over to unlock the case.

"Ooh!" Hannah gasped. It looked even prettier out from under the grubby glass.

"It's perfect, isn't it?"

Hannah took it from the woman and set it against her dress. "Look! Right here, on the hip. That would be amazing, huh?"

"Yeah!" I smiled at how well it looked above the soft ruffles in the skirt. "The pin looks like it was made for the dress."

"I know. I love it!" Hannah giggled. "Holy cow, I'm going to be a total knockout at the party."

"Yeah, you're gonna look amazing."

"Too bad you aren't coming. You've got to see the other dress I found over there. I think it would look marvelous on you."

"What? Are you kidding?"

"No. Come on, I'll show you."

I followed Hannah back to the tall, circular rack that held the vintage gowns, mostly from the 1980s and 1990s. *Yuck!*

"Here it is!"

I stared at the shimmering, pale gold gown she pulled out. It was total 1940s, but elegant-lounge-singer-type '40s. "Wow! That is pretty."

"Yeah, I thought it would go perfect with your blond hair."

Dang! It probably would. "Oh." *Okay, so now I really wish I'd gotten an invite. What's the deal, anyway? I invited Cassidy and Claire to my party. Even though I would probably say no, they could've at least been nice and asked.* I touched the smooth satin of the dress with my index finger. *Maybe dressing up wouldn't be that bad after all.*

A couple of days later, I felt even worse about not getting invited when Chase came over to ask what something on his invitation meant. *Good grief! He got invited too?*

"So do you have any idea what this is about?" He grinned boyishly at me across the countertop while I stirred the dough for Mom's to-die-for chocolate-chip cookies. "I mean, I don't have to dress up, do I?"

"You? Worried about dressing up?" I smirked as I gave the dough a final stir. "I thought you liked costumes."

He rolled his eyes. "Only if they're made of armor."

I laughed and shook my head, then ducked down to pull out a couple of my mother's stoneware cookie sheets.

"No, honestly, do I have to wear some 1940s Mafia outfit?"

"Yeah, I think so. That's what Hannah's doing."

"Wait, where's your invite? Maybe something was left off mine. Does yours clarify the costume thing?"

I stood and placed the cookie sheets on the counter. Not ready to answer him, I walked over to the silverware drawer and pulled out two spoons. When I came back I handed one to him. "Here, make yourself useful."

"You sure? I'm not the best cook, you know. I mean, I've been known to have a whole batch of cookies disappear right in front of me—before they make it into the oven."

"Disappear? What are you—?"

Chase stuck a spoonful of cookie dough in his mouth. "Mmm. Your mom always did have the best recipes."

I put my hands on my hips. "Chase Anderson, you are *not* going to devour all of the cookie dough!"

"Okay." He smiled mischievously as he dipped his spoon in for another bite. "I promise I won't eat it *all.*"

"Eww! That's totally double dipping." I could hear him chuckling to himself as I stomped over to the cabinet and grabbed a small dessert plate. "Here." I hurried back and used my clean spoon to remove the contaminated portion of the dough and set it on the plate. "This is yours, okay? Sheesh! Can you promise to behave yourself now?"

Chase gave me a fake humble look, then dug into his plate for another bite of dough. "Thanks."

"Guys! Are you all like this?" I asked as I put a spoonful of dough on the first cookie sheet. "Because if you are, I don't think I want a boyfriend after all."

Chase shrugged while fishing for a chocolate chip on his plate. "Yeah, as far as I know, all guys are like this." He plopped the tiny chocolate piece in his mouth and grinned.

I sighed and quickly spooned more dough onto the stone before Chase could finish his off and start on the rest.

He watched me and then asked, "What does your invite say?"

For crying out loud, are we back to that again? I worked intently on finishing up a row of dough dollops as I answered matter-of-factly, "I didn't get one."

I heard a clatter as he dropped his spoon on the countertop. "What do you mean?" he asked.

I shrugged and focused on dropping small spoonfuls of dough onto the sheet. "That I didn't get invited."

"Yeah, but why?" he persisted.

I finished that stone and moved to the empty one. "I don't know. Maybe Cassidy knew I would tell her no, so she didn't bother inviting me."

Chase snorted. "That's crazy. Like you wouldn't go to her party. You love parties—of course you'd go."

I looked up at him and raised an eyebrow, then dipped my spoon in the bowl for another glob of dough.

"Emma, you're kidding, aren't you?"

"What makes you think I'm kidding?" I kept working. "Why would I go to a costume party just because Cassidy has invited me?"

"Because you're nice."

"What does that mean?" I glanced up at him.

For a very long moment, he stared at me. His eyes searched through mine, behind the layers of hurt I had hidden there. I couldn't move. Finally, he looked down and released me. The corner of his mouth drooped slightly and his brows furrowed.

I cleared my throat and quickly plopped more cookie dough onto his plate. "Here. I better give you this before you try to steal some more."

Chase looked at it and grinned. "Thanks." He took another chunk and slowly licked it off the spoon.

After I filled the second cookie sheet without another word from him, I realized he must be contemplating something. I carried the stones one at a time, set them in the oven, and started the timer. Another couple of minutes saw the counter cleaned off and the dishes in the sink so I could wash them later. When I finished, I walked back over to the counter and leaned on it, watching Chase savor his last bite of cookie dough. I couldn't stand it anymore. "Okay, so tell me what you're thinking. You're driving me crazy."

"I am?" he said devilishly.

I picked up the plate and took the empty spoon from his hand. "Yes!"

As I walked over to the sink, I got my answer. I wished I'd never asked.

TWELVE

♥

Stop, drop, and roll, baby. You're on fire!

"I've been thinking you should get to know Cassidy better," Chase said.

What? I flipped around. "Cassidy?"

"Yeah. Why not?"

I walked back to the counter where he sat. "You want me to get to know Cassidy Hart better? Why?"

"I think you two could be really good friends."

"Cassidy and me? Are you crazy? No way."

Chase had the audacity to smile, like he thought it was funny. "I think you two would get along great."

"Maybe, but there's just something about her that gets on my nerves. She's not rude or anything—she's just . . . she's . . ." *Annoying.* "I don't know. We're just very different, that's all."

"Really? I think you two are a lot alike."

"Ha! Whatever. You so can't read people as well as you think, if you think Cassidy and I are alike. I'm not sure if I should be offended by that or not."

"Why should you be offended?" Chase asked. "I meant it as a compliment."

I rolled my eyes.

"Come on, Em. You really don't see the similarities?"

I snorted, then walked over to the sink and began to wash the dishes. Letting the hot, soapy water fill up one side, I glanced back and said, "Just for curiosity's sake, I would like to hear one—just one—thing you think Cassidy and I have in common."

"Okay." Chase walked around the counter and leaned his hip against the side closest to me. "You wanna know what you have in common? I'll tell you."

I turned off the sink, then faced him and folded my arms.

One corner of his mouth turned up. "Well, for starters you're both blond."

"That's the best you can—"

"And," he interrupted, "you're both really artistic."

"Artistic? What in the—?"

"Okay. You may not think photography is an art, but I do. Just because Cassidy doesn't use a paintbrush to capture images, doesn't mean it isn't art."

"Okay, fine. You're right. I forgot she was a photographer. But that's not enough—"

"That's not enough? Okay then. You both love to throw parties."

I rolled my eyes. *Now he's really desperate.* I picked up the dishcloth, then put the large bowl into the water and started to scrub.

"Hey! I'm not done," Chase said. "You both have eccentric mothers. You both like the same movies. You both used to have a crush on my little brother, Taylor—"

"What? I did not!" I spun around, flinging soapy water with me.

A couple of splats landed on Chase's shirt. "Hey, watch it." He laughed and stepped toward the end of the counter.

"I have *never* had a crush on your little brother. As if!"

"Really?" Chase's smile was way too confident. He walked over to my mom's address book, near the phone on the counter against the wall. He picked up the book.

Dang!

Heading toward me, he flipped to the last page. "Let's see here. Hmm, right underneath 'Business Contacts.' Yep, here it is—small, I grant you, but definitely legible. "'Emma plus Taylor equals true love forever.' You even used plus and equal signs, and a cute little number '4' instead of 'for' in 'forever.'"

My face flamed. "Give that back!" I went to snatch the address book out of Chase's hand, but he was too quick for me.

"No, no, no! Wait! There's more."

"Chase Lionel Anderson!" I tried to grab it again.

He deftly dodged my hand and held the book high above his head. "Uh-oh! You *are* embarrassed. Middle names, even. Well, two can play at that game, Miss Emmalee Elaine Bradford. Or wait! Should I say Mrs. Emmalee *Anderson?*"

Ugh! "You're not even funny, Chase." I jumped up and tried to reach the stupid book, but he was just too tall. Besides, it only made him laugh louder.

"What? I thought you wanted to be called that," he said. "That's what you wrote."

I couldn't help it. I grinned. "You're horrible—you know that, right?"

"Yeah, actually, I've been told that a few times." His eyes twinkled a moment and I suddenly realized how close I was to him.

Hurriedly, I took a step back. With my face still red, I went to work again, fiercely scrubbing the remaining utensils and measuring cups.

Chase must've realized the game was over, because he walked over to the counter next to me and tossed the address book on it. "There. You can have it. I think I got my point across." He chuckled again. "So you want me to tell you what else you and Cassidy have in common?"

"Nah, I'm good." I rinsed the utensils. After setting them on a dishtowel to dry, I turned toward Chase. "You sure seemed to know a lot about Cassidy. Do you like her or something?"

"Like her? No, not in the way you're thinking. I just worry about her, that's all."

"Do you hang out at her house a lot?" For some reason, it bothered me that he might feel just as comfortable at her place as he did at mine.

"No, not a lot. But I am trying to get to know the family Taylor hopes to be part of one day."

"Yes, I knew he was going to marry her." I beamed proudly.

"Ah! So I see you don't have a crush on him anymore."

"What? No. Like I would." I giggled. "That was so two years ago. I'm way over Taylor Anderson now."

"Good. I'm glad to hear it." Chase grinned, and I wondered briefly what else he was thinking but not telling me.

Three days later and two days before the party, there was a knock on my front door. I opened it and stared at a clearly embarrassed Cassidy Hart.

"Hi," I gasped.

She glanced behind me and smiled slightly. "Can we talk? Do you mind if I come in?"

"Oh! Uh, sure." I stepped back and opened the door wider. "Come on in."

"Thanks."

She walked hesitantly into the house and I poked my head outside. "Is Claire coming?" I asked.

"No." Cassidy paused. "I—I walked here."

"You walked here? Are you kidding me? How far is that?"

"I dunno, like three miles or something."

What? And they let her walk that far alone? Cassidy must've read my mind, because she said, "It's all I'm allowed to do by myself—walk."

Wow! I was so surprised it took me a moment to realize this was probably the most I had ever heard Cassidy speak in at least two years. "You want to talk in here?" I asked, wondering why she was there. I pointed toward the front room and then followed her. I waited until she chose a sofa before sitting across from her.

She took a deep breath and shakily smiled again. "You're probably wondering why I'm here, aren't you?"

"The thought has crossed my mind." I grinned to take the sting out of my words.

"Well, it's to apologize, actually."

"Apologize?"

"Here." Cassidy pulled an envelope out of her pocket. "I guess I got the house number wrong. This—this is for you." She leaned forward to hand it to me.

I took the envelope and saw "Return to Sender," scrawled in bold letters across the front. *My invitation! I did get one.*

Cassidy was quick to explain. "When that came in the mail after school, I was sick to my stomach. I mean, I know it's no big deal, really. It's just a stupid party I'm throwing this weekend. And I know you will more than likely not want to

117

come anyway. It's just, it's just . . . I didn't want you to feel left out, you know? Especially when a lot of people you know will be there. Anyway, I had to walk straight here and give it to you. I know it's last minute and all, but you are welcome to come."

"Oh, thank you." I opened the invitation and pulled it out. "It looks like fun."

"Really?" Cassidy smiled hopefully. "I'm kind of worried about it. My sister Chloe used to do these amazing parties every year with her friends. This is my first attempt, so I am kind of nervous."

"Oh," I said, not sure what else to say. It wasn't that I was speechless in Cassidy's presence, I was just so thrown off by her candor. *Say something already,* I told myself. "So who's all coming, do you know?"

"From what it looks like, almost everyone I've invited."

"You said people I know will be there?"

"Oh, yeah. Definitely."

Yes, but who did you invite? I tried another tactic. "I know Chase is going. And I heard earlier that Carson and his girlfriend were coming. Do you have anyone else older coming to the party, or is everyone else from school?"

"Well, Ethan Franklin, Carson's little brother, said he might drive up from Albuquerque to come."

No way! I forced myself not to hyperventilate. "Really? Hmm, that would be nice. Do you know him well?"

"Yeah, we're friends."

I leaned toward Cassidy. "So what's he like? Is he funny? Is he as cool as everybody says?"

"He seems pretty cool."

"Do you think he's cute? I've heard people say he's pretty hot. What do you think?"

118

Cassidy looked away. "Yeah, I've heard people say that too."

"Yeah, but what do *you* think about him? I've never met him before, and I'm dying to know what he's like."

She shrugged her shoulders. "He definitely seems very nice, and a lot of people like to hang around with him."

"Yeah, but what does he look like?"

"He looks nice."

Ugh! Now I remember why Cassidy gets on my nerves. Can't the girl answer a question without sounding like a politician? For crying out loud, I get more response from Lady's puppies. I smiled sweetly. "Well, I guess I'll have to see for myself when I come to the party."

Cassidy's jaw dropped. "Y–you're coming?"

Uh, did I say that out loud? "Sure. You don't want me to come?"

"No—I mean yes! You're definitely welcome. You're more than welcome. I was just surprised. You didn't even have a chance to really look at the invite."

"Yeah, well, I've seen Hannah's, so I already knew all about it."

"Now I feel even worse," Cassidy moaned.

I chuckled. "Don't worry about it. It's no big deal, really. I understand. Accidents happen."

"Thanks." She smiled. There was a pause before she clapped her hands on her knees and said, "Well, I need to be heading home. Should I write your name on the RSVP list then?"

Great. What have I gotten myself into? "Yep. Make sure I'm on it." I stood up when she did. "Do you need me to bring anything?"

Cassidy positively beamed. "No, but thank you for asking. That was really sweet of you."

Nice. Someone else who thinks I'm a snob. Am I ever gonna change my reputation? "No problem." I walked her to the door and added, "Just let me know if you change your mind and think of some way I can help."

"Thank you, I will."

I watched as she stepped out into the bright sunshine. "Do you need a ride? I can drive you home."

"No!" I was surprised by the vehemence in her voice, but she quickly softened it and explained, "I like to walk, really. As I said before, it's my chance to be alone."

I wouldn't want to take away someone's alone time, especially their alone time from Claire. "Well, I hope you enjoy your walk."

"Thanks. I will. Bye!"

"Bye."

I watched Cassidy head down the driveway and marveled a bit at what life must be like for her at home. I had heard stories about her mom but had never met her. *Hmm, I wonder if she'll be at the party. Who am I kidding? I wonder if* Ethan *will be there!*

THIRTEEN

♥

Didn't I see you on the cover of Vogue?

Ethan didn't show up at Cassidy's party. It was the first thing I heard when I walked into the Harts' home that weekend. Apparently, he had a test to study for. Judging by the disappointed faces around me, it looked like quite a few people were looking forward to seeing him. *Ugh. This party is going to be so stupid*, I thought. *Why did I even waste my time coming here, seriously?*

I guess I didn't do a very good job hiding my frustration, because Chase came up behind me and whispered, "Hey, you don't have to pout. Ethan will show up sooner or later."

I clenched my teeth, then recovered and turned around. "I wasn't pouting. But thank you, Chase, for being such a gentleman and pointing out that you thought so. Nothing like telling a girl she looks funny."

"Hey! I never said anything about your looks. Which are very nice, by the way. Where did you find that costume? Did you rent it?"

"You like my lounge-singer dress, eh?" I twirled around to show off the whole ensemble. *I mean, if the guy is giving away compliments, he might as well be giving them to me.*

"Very pretty. You look like you stepped out of a Bob Hope movie."

Bob Hope? Who's that? "I . . . is that a good thing?"

"Don't tell me you have no idea who the great Bob Hope is."

"Okay, I won't."

Chase sighed. "I practically grew up on his movies. He was my grandpa's favorite movie star and comedian."

"So he's funny, too?"

Chase looked at me like I was from another planet.

"What? I've never heard of the guy, so sue me, okay?" I was saved from Chase's undoubtedly rude response when Hannah ran up.

"Emma! You're here. Wow, that dress makes you look like a million bucks!"

"Thanks." I smiled. "Yours looks great, too. That brooch turned out perfect."

"Oh! Have you seen Cassidy's costume?" Hannah gushed. "If you think ours look good, just wait until you see hers."

"Really?"

"It looks amazing."

I glanced over at Chase to read his reaction. He nodded his head. "Yeah, she looks really good," he said. "I think she blows every other costume here out of the water."

"Oh. That's cool." I couldn't quite put my finger on why Cassidy's costume being so great bothered me, but it did. That was until I saw it. *Holy cow!* Chase was right. It totally blew away Hannah's and my '80s knockoffs. Cassidy wore a vintage 1940s dress. An antique. And it fit her like a glove. After several speechless seconds as I watched her walk into the kitchen and mingle with a couple of guests, I approached her.

"Cassidy, I love your dress. Where did you get it?"

She smiled and glanced down at it. "Thank you. It was my great-grandma's."

"Your great-grandma's? Are you kidding? And you're allowed to wear it."

She laughed. "It's actually falling apart. Don't look too close or you'll see spots where the sequins and rhinestones are missing. I've been patching it up for weeks, getting it ready for tonight."

Should you really wear valuable antiques that are falling apart? "But—"

Cassidy laughed again. "Don't worry. I have a whole storage container full of her old dresses. She used to perform a lot, so she had a lot of cool clothes. This is by far the worst of the lot. You should see some of the other gowns."

"Really?"

"Yeah. When I was little and she came to visit, I always dressed up in my mom's clothes. Granny wasn't sure what to do with her old things, so she willed them to me. They came with specific instructions that said I wasn't supposed to sell them or hide them away. I was supposed to 'dress up' and show them off, just like I did with my mom's clothes when I was younger. If it wasn't for Granny, I don't think I would've been able to convince my mom to let me throw this party to begin with."

"Cass, Mom needs you," interrupted Claire. "She's in the family room trying to decide how many teams there will be. So can you go and tell her how many people are here? Oh! You made the punch. Good. I like that punch. Ooh! Emmalee, your dress is so— Don't you think her dress is pretty, Cass? Cass? Oh, duh, she's heading over to help my mom. I totally forgot already. Have you tried any cookies, Emma? Cass made them.

They're really . . . here, you have to try them. Cassidy is the best baker ever. They're her very own recipe."

"Thank you." I took a cookie and looked around for an escape. But Claire was quicker than I was.

"When did you get here? You're so nice for coming—we didn't think you would. You have no idea how surprised we were when Cass came back from your house saying you were coming. But even then, my mom said she'd be shocked if you really showed up. I told her how nice you were and how you were so fun at your party. Hey, I liked the pizza at your party. Was that Little Caesar's? I can't remember. It was good, though! My mom said she would have to wait and see how you acted here—if you came—before she would form her opinion of you, since she's positive you'll say something rude. Oh! I wasn't supposed to tell you that! Well, you won't tell my mom, will you? Of course you won't. You're too nice, remember? Oh, look! There's my friend Jared. I hope you don't mind if I leave you to go talk to him. I've been waiting for him to show up this whole time. Jared! Jared—"

Whew! Saved by Jared. Dazed, I watched Claire's beeline toward the poor guy. Just then, I heard a familiar chuckle behind me.

I grinned and closed my eyes a moment before turning around. "Chase, it is not nice to laugh at me."

"Who says I was laughing at you?" His blue eyes sparkled playfully into my own. "I was thinking of the poor guy Claire just herded into that corner."

Chase's eyes were way too pretty. It seriously wasn't fair. "So how are you holding up?" I asked. "I mean, talk about awkward. This is totally a high school party. Could there be more measly little teenagers in one place? Honestly. You've got to be the oldest guy here, so—"

The rest of what I was about to say was smothered by Chase's finger over my mouth. Before I could react, he propelled me through a small doorway next to the kitchen, down a step into the laundry room. *What in the—?* He shut the door. We were all alone.

"Will you stop?"

I was stunned by the anger in his voice. "What do you mean?"

Chase took a couple of swift steps toward the large washing machine and turned around. He roughly ran his hand over his face, then took a deep breath.

"Stop what, Chase? What did I say?" I was beginning to get worried.

"Look, you don't always have to be a prom queen, okay?"

Prom queen?

"Sometimes it's okay to go somewhere and just enjoy a place for what it is. You know—relax, have fun, and not always expect everything to be super great entertainment."

Where in the world did this come from?

"To answer your question," he said, "yes, I'm having a fabulous time, all right?"

"O-kay?"

"And yes, I may be the oldest guy here, but so far I've met some pretty cool people." He pushed himself away from the washer and approached me. "Many of them, believe it or not, I already know, because they work for my dad. Now if you'll excuse me, I'm going back to the party, which is ten times more fun than being in here with you."

"Chase?" But I spoke to thin air. He had already opened the door and left. Baffled and hurt, I slowly walked over to the washing machine and absentmindedly let my fingers trail over the lid.

Why am I even here, anyway? I knew coming to this party would be a big mistake. I even dressed up in a costume, for goodness sake! I never wear costumes. Am I really the only one who feels uncomfortable playing dress-up? I thought of Hannah and Cassidy, both of them happy with the large crowd of people out there. If I was honest with myself, I hardly knew anyone at the party. And for the first time in my life, I felt utterly alone.

I stared blankly at the other door, which led to the Harts' carport. When two crummy tears started to make their way past my heavily lined lashes, I knew this whole party was a waste. In a flash, I opened the side door and walked outside. I prayed my heels would last as I gingerly made my way down the gravel driveway toward my car. There were so many people at the party; it wasn't like I'd be missed. Besides, there was no reason to stay anyway.

Three weeks later, Hannah still hadn't forgiven me for bolting from the party. I hadn't realized she would actually miss me that much, and it was kind of gratifying to find out she had, even though I had tried to block that night from my memory. It's not pretty reliving messy eyeliner streaks and stupid costumes that refuse to come off fast enough.

So I cried. Big deal. I must've been just highly emotional that day or something. Anyway, I probably would've done a pretty good job of blocking out my memories of the party, had Hannah not insisted on bringing it up every couple of hours or so.

"I'll never forgive you—ever—for leaving that party," she announced as we walked through the grocery store with my mom's last-minute Thanksgiving shopping list.

"So you've said. A thousand times, I might add." I stopped and grabbed two cans of black olives and one jar of green ones. I set the cans in the cart and crossed them off the list.

"Yes, but it's true. I can't forgive you."

I sighed, then looked at the list again. The next line read, "Crackers and cheese." I headed for the cracker aisle. Hannah followed.

"Really, I don't think you realize what a fool I looked like searching for you," she said. "I mean, my goodness, I thought you had got locked in one of the Harts' bathrooms or something. How was I supposed to know you had just up and decided to leave like that? Didn't you even think how rude you might look to people?"

We turned into the cracker aisle and I searched for my mom's favorite crackers. "No, Hannah. I didn't think about coming off as rude. Honestly, I wasn't trying to ruin the party for you, okay?"

"Well, why did you leave then?"

There it was. The question I didn't want anyone, even Hannah, to know the answer to. But how could I tell her I left because Chase didn't want to be around me, and because Mrs. Hart was waiting for me to say or do something rude to prove I wasn't nice? Or even worse, that I left because Chase made me cry? It was something I didn't want to admit to anyone, including myself. It didn't matter anyway, because Chase was right. I did think I was better than everyone there. I wasn't at the party to enjoy myself; I was there to meet Ethan Franklin, plain and simple. But if I'd given the party half a chance, I might've actually had fun. I mean, I was warming up and I was pretty curious about the games they were planning. *Ugh!* But who was I kidding? No one had really wanted me to be at the party. They hadn't expected me to show up at all.

"Hey, Emma!" A voice interrupted my thoughts.

It was Carson Franklin. "Oh, hi! I didn't see you there." I smiled and then glanced at the guy by his side. He was really cute and staring straight at me.

"Imagine running into you at Safeway, of all places." Carson nudged the guy next to him in the arm. "Ethan, that's Emmalee Bradford, the girl I've been telling you about."

FOURTEEN

♥

Well, here I am. What were your other two wishes?

Eeeh! My heart skipped a beat as I returned Ethan's easy smile. "Hello," I said shyly.

Suddenly, his grin grew to dangerously enchanting proportions, and I was struck by the wicked gleam in his hazel eyes. He took a step toward my cart and then another to the side of it. Then, he pulled the cart—and me along with it—right up to him and said, "Hey yourself."

I held on to the cart for dear life and willed my knees not to buckle. Ethan's playful eyes held no secrets, and I could tell he knew exactly the sort of effect he had on me. I stared at the cleft in his chin and felt my face go red. Ethan chuckled—the scoundrel.

Carson saved me. "Hannah, I don't think you've met my little brother, either."

I watched Ethan use his charm on Hannah as he answered her greeting. "Hi. You're Emma's friend, right?" His profile showed hints of a five o'clock shadow. I tried hard not to stare at his firm jaw that was, even now, graced by a smile for Hannah. His gaze and mine collided again, and before I could look away he winked.

He is way too flirtatious for his own good. Guys like that should not be allowed out in public. Clearly, he thought I would fall at his feet. I decided to give him a run for his money. I picked a couple of boxes of random crackers and tossed them into the cart. "Well, it was nice meeting you, uh— What was your name again? Ian?"

"Ethan." The devilish grin morphed into a full-out smirk, his perfect teeth set off by his tan skin.

"Ethan, that's right. Sorry. It was really nice to meet you. I hope you enjoy Thanksgiving in a couple of days." I turned to Carson and beamed my Bradford smile right at him. In my peripheral vision, I caught Ethan stepping back in shock, and Carson's jaw dropped right in front of me. "Excuse us," I said flippantly as we started walking away. As a parting shot, I added, "Don't forget to have Madison call me, Carson. I would love to get together with her and do something. Bye."

"She knows Madison, too?" I heard Ethan mutter as I turned the corner toward the dairy aisle.

Hannah jogged up to the cart. "Why did you leave?" She looked baffled. "Ethan was totally hitting on you. I thought you've wanted to meet him for forever. And now you just leave? I don't get it."

I laughed and shook my head. "He'll be back, I promise."

He was back a lot sooner than I thought. The next day— Wednesday—after school, Ethan and Carson showed up at my house with Madison in tow.

"Hey, we were wondering if you wanted to hit the trails for a bit before dinner," Carson said.

I was lost. "Hit the trails?"

Ethan dangled his keys in front of me. "Yeah, you know, four wheelin'?"

Wow! "Are you for real?"

Madison laughed. "Sure, why not? There's room for four in Ethan's Jeep."

I had to think fast. "Um, sure, yeah. Hang on. Let me run and tell my mom. You guys are welcome to come on in." I opened the door wider but they all protested, obviously eager to go. I sighed. "Okay, give me a minute and I'll be back." I left the door slightly ajar and walked into the kitchen, where I had been helping my mom cook for tomorrow's Thanksgiving dinner. "Hey, Mom?"

"Yes?"

"Carson and Ethan Franklin are at the door with Madison Coolidge. They were wondering if I could go four-wheeling with them for a bit before dinner."

"Is Chase going too?"

I still didn't have the heart to tell my mom I hadn't heard from Chase since the Halloween party. "No, I don't think so."

"Well, why don't you invite him?"

"But Mom, I'm sure there are a hundred other things he would rather be doing than hanging out with me and my friends."

Mom set a bowl down and walked over to the counter. "Emma, the Franklin brothers are older than you."

"So?"

"So, I would feel better about it if you invited Chase along."

Holy cow. How humiliating. "There's not room for Chase, Mom. Besides, this is Ethan Franklin we're talking about, the best four-wheel driver in all of New Mexico. I'm perfectly safe with him."

"She's right, ma'am." I was caught off guard by Ethan's deep voice behind me. I whipped my head around. He was alone and standing in the doorway. "I would never do anything to put your daughter's life at risk. Believe me, when she's with me, she'll always be perfectly safe."

As he walked up to me, I turned to see if his charm had worked on my mom.

She looked from him to me and then back again. "Were you there in Moab last summer, Ethan, when Kylie Russell had her accident that now has her in a wheelchair?"

He flinched, then lowered his eyes and said, "Yes."

"Were you in charge then? Were you around when she broke her neck and nearly died?" my mother spat.

Whoa. I had never seen my mom so freaked out before.

"I—" Ethan glanced at her and then at me. I watched his eyes cloud with emotion as he stared right into mine and answered, "Yes. I was in charge." He looked over at my mother and said firmly, "Believe me, it will never happen again."

"No, it won't. Emma, you're not going," my mom said firmly.

"What?"

"You can stay here and help me with tomorrow's dinner."

"But I—" Mom's look stopped me. She was dead serious. And I was mortified. *Can I just shrivel up and die, please? Really, anytime now is good. Why are mothers so embarrassing?*

Ethan handled it better than I thought he would—better than, I'm sure, my mom thought he would. In fact, all he did was clear his throat and nod before saying, "O-kay. That settles that. I guess I'll be off then. I'll let you know if we plan things that are less dangerous. It was nice meeting you, Mrs. Bradford."

"I'll walk you to the door," I said. When we were out of earshot I added, "Thanks for thinking of me, really. I would've liked to have gone. Sorry my mom was so—well, protective."

"Hey, no worries. Just be grateful she loves you as much as she does."

I let out a short bark of laughter and rolled my eyes. "Yeah, a little too much! I'm the baby of the family. I get babied a lot."

Ethan just looked at me for a moment, then said, "Well, Carson won't be too happy. He was looking forward to all of us hitting the hills. I guess that's what we get for planning stuff so last minute . . ." Ethan's voice trailed off as we approached the door.

Carson beamed at me. "So are we all ready to go?"

"Uh . . ." I looked at Ethan.

He quickly covered for me. "Emma can't make it. She promised her mom she'd help cook Thanksgiving dinner."

Madison and Carson both looked disappointed. "Really? You can't get out of it?" Carson asked.

I smiled weakly. "I tried." I watched an "I'll tell you later" look pass between the brothers and wished I hadn't. "Well, thanks for coming by. Maybe we can do something another time. Do you need my cell number?"

"Ethan, why don't you put Emma's digits in your phone?" Carson said. "Oh, hey, Emma, I just met a real cool guy and his girlfriend. He's a senior this year at Farmington High, but his girlfriend goes to Pedra Vista. Maybe you know him. Does the name Elton Bloomfield ring a bell?"

Elton has a girlfriend? What is poor Hannah going to think?
"Yeah, I know him."

"Cool! I was thinking we might all head to the movies one night—like a whole group of us, while Ethan's in town. What do ya say?"

"With Elton?" *No way.* "Sure. Ethan can text or call me when y'all come up with definite plans." *Hopefully they'll forget all about it.*

After dithering with Ethan's cell phone, they left. A few minutes later, someone pounded on the door. I opened it and there stood Hannah.

"Oh my gosh! Oh my gosh! Oh my GOSH!" she said as she paced in the foyer.

Dang. She knows about Elton. "What? What is it? Did you hear?" I led her into the front room.

She sighed and sat for a moment before bolting out of her chair and walking over to the fireplace.

"Hannah? Did something happen?"

She nervously touched the porcelain figurine on the mantel. She turned toward me and gasped. "I saw him!"

"Elton?"

She frowned. "No, not Elton. I saw Martin. Just now!"

"Oh?" *Oh, dang it.* "Where were you? Was he rude or something?"

She fidgeted with her hands and then ran them through her hair before she walked up to the couch where I stood. "No, no. He wasn't rude, not at all. That's what I don't get. I know he hates me. Why doesn't he just treat me like dirt and get on with it?" She slumped down on the sofa and put her head in her hands.

Cautiously, I lowered myself onto the cushion next to her. "So what happened?"

Hannah mumbled something I couldn't quite make out before she sat up and looked right at me. "Okay, here goes." She took a deep breath. "So my mom made me take her car and run to the store for her, because she forgot rolls and cranberry sauce for tomorrow. So while I was there, I saw Martin shopping with his mom. I totally freaked out—you have no idea. Anyway, I ducked behind a huge tower of cereal so he wouldn't see me. I would've totally taken off, except I panicked and left the stupid shopping cart in the middle of the aisle—and it had my purse in it. So I couldn't leave it, you know?"

I grinned. "No, definitely not."

"Well, Martin walked right up to the cart and noticed my purse. Why do I carry yellow purses? Honestly, you'd think I'd learn better. He must've known it was mine, because I saw him looking around. That's when he spotted me. Talk about giving me a heart attack. I quickly pretended to be considering the cereal I was hiding behind, but I can't even tell you what brand it was. Anyway, he walked right up to me. Oh my gosh, I thought I would die. I tried to look cool reading the info on the boxes, but when he stood next to me and said hi, I lost it. Seriously. I jerked up and like an idiot knocked over like half of the tower, right on the guy, too! Boxes of cereal went everywhere and people had to stop their carts and everything to watch me pick it up."

"Really?" I said, trying not to laugh.

"Why does stuff like this happen to me, Emma? I mean, like, couldn't I have just gone into the store and bought the two things my mom asked me to without acting like a complete idiot?"

"So what happened?" I asked.

Hannah sighed. "Well, I picked up as many boxes as I could as fast as I could without causing even more of a scene."

"No, I mean with Martin."

"He was the perfect gentleman, like always. He stayed and helped me pick them up, and when we were done he acted like he was going to say something. But I was so embarrassed my only thought was to get out of there as soon as possible. So I quickly shoved a bunch of the boxes into my cart, said thank you, and hightailed it out of the store. I drove straight here. I had to talk to you!"

"Wait. Did you finish your shopping for your mom?"

"With him there? Are you kidding?" Hannah looked at me like I had grown horns. "No, I just bought the cereal. I figured I'll wait a few more minutes and then go back once the coast is clear."

"That makes sense."

"So tell me something—anything—to make me forget what a total dork I was just now."

"Anything? Are you sure?" I asked.

"Yeah, I don't care what it is. Just distract me, please."

"Well, uh, Elton's got a new girlfriend. And she's from Pedra Vista High."

FIFTEEN

♥

I hope you know CPR, cuz you take my breath away!

Okay, so maybe that wasn't the perfect time to bring up
Elton. But desperate times call for desperate measures.
Hannah needed a distraction, the poor girl—what else was I
supposed to do? As it was, she was in more of a mess when
she left than when she'd arrived. I had no idea she was still
crushing on Elton that hard. *Sheesh, the guy totally burned
her.* I guess it's tough when you've liked someone as long as
she liked him.

My night of errors didn't end there, either. Just when I
thought things couldn't get worse, Chase came over. I don't
usually whine about the injustices of life, but honestly! Were
the Fates determined to see me crack? Like my mom freaking
out and embarrassing Ethan wasn't bad enough. Then there
was the whole Hannah–Elton blunder right afterwards. But
having to deal with Chase the same night really was not
fair.

"Hey, can I come in?" he said when I answered the door.

Sure. Why not? Might as well join the party. "Yeah, I'm helping my mom in the kitchen. Is there something you need?" I stepped back and let him walk into the house.

He had a sheepish grin on his face. "Actually, I need to see you."

"I thought you didn't want to be in the same room as me."

At least he had the decency to wince. "Look. Can we talk?"

"You're sure you want to hear what I have to say?" I said, walking into the front room Hannah had just vacated. "This room isn't too confining for you, is it?"

"Emma, stop. This isn't like you."

"What isn't like me?" I smiled my Bradford smile.

Chase stared at me wearily before nodding his head. "I deserved that."

Ooh! Why does he irritate me so much?

"I came here to apologize. I would've been here before now, but I've been away helping my dad with his offices in Durango."

"Y–you've been away?" Concerned, I took a couple of steps toward Chase, before I realized what I was doing and stopped.

He moved closer. "Yeah, and I've felt . . . I've . . . Look, I didn't mean it, okay? What I said at Cassidy's party was uncalled for. There were many different ways I could've gotten my point across, but I didn't and I'm sorry. I definitely didn't mean for you to leave the party."

His eyes tugged at mine and I felt my anger begin to melt. After a few seconds of silence, I admitted, "You were right, though. I did think I was better than everyone else. And I definitely didn't go to the party to be entertained and to have a good time. But I was surprised once I got there." I looked up at him. "Really surprised. And I know I didn't act exactly like I should've, but I . . . uh, was okay with being there."

"Then why did you leave?" He searched my face, making me lower my head. "Em?" He put two fingers under my chin and gently raised it. "Did you leave because of me?"

I quickly turned my head away. In the next instant, he wrapped his arms around me and pulled me against his muscular form. My cheek rested on his sports jacket, and I could make out the faintest smell of Hugo Boss cologne.

All of a sudden, Chase seemed different. My senses were in such a muddle, I couldn't put my finger on what it was.

"Sorry, Em. I'm really sorry."

His deep voice above my head sent a shiver of sparks down my spine. I became aware of his heartbeat thudding beneath my ear. *This is so weird.* Ever so gently, so as not to hurt his feelings, I pulled away and straightened up my clothing. "No worries. I'm fine." I tried to laugh and pass it off as if nothing had happened. But something *had* happened.

"Are you sure?" He brought his arm up to hold my shoulder and I stepped back from him.

"Yeah, I—I'm positive. Everything is fine." *Everything is not fine.*

"Okay, well, if you say so." He looked just as uncomfortable as I felt, and for a second I took pity on him.

Snap out of it. It's Chase. You've known him your whole life. So why are you acting like he's a stranger or something? "Are you coming over for dinner tomorrow with your family?" I asked.

"Uh, yeah. It's your mom's turn to host it, isn't it? I should be there."

"She's really excited. She's been cooking up a storm."

"Just like every time, I'll bet."

Why are we talking about my mom? "So, I guess I better go in and help her."

"Oh, yep. Uh, I'll see myself out. Thanks for listening." He ducked his head and grinned at me.

"No problem." I smiled. "Ditto."

His smile fell as he stared at my mouth. Then he cleared his throat and said, "Well, I'll see you tomorrow."

"Bye."

He was out the front door before I had a chance to leave the room.

Thanksgiving Dinner was much better than I expected. Luckily, the unease I had felt around Chase the night before had all but vanished. He came early and helped my dad set up the table and chairs to create a formal dining room, while my mom and I were peeling the potatoes. I was impressed when Chase asked if he could lay out the tablecloth and silverware, too. When I saw the finished product about thirty minutes later, I was even more impressed. The table looked amazing. At some point, he had even brought over a beautiful floral centerpiece.

"Let me guess. You took a few culinary arts classes in Spain."

He laughed. "What? No." He pointed to the elegant table. "Dad made me work in his restaurant for a year. They were real sticklers—everything had to be just right. I have never known such a finicky manager as the one Dad hired for that restaurant."

"Really?" I walked around the table and touched one of the dessert spoons—there were two at each plate. "You really know how to set all of these in order like that? That's really cool." My fingers glided over my mother's white and gold china plates and then lingered on the rows of beautifully crafted silver utensils. "Mom's had this silver for years and we've never used the whole set before." I laughed as I read my name on one of mom's Regency place cards. "Now I know why. She was probably terrified in case your parents saw that she didn't know what everything was used for, or where to place it."

"It's not hard, once you get the hang of it." Chase shrugged. "Just between you and me, my dad's never worked in his restaurant before. Neither of my parents know how to lay the silverware either. That's why they used to make me do it." Chase straightened a knife that was a bit off kilter. "I bet they would've never known the difference, to tell the truth. There's a difference between knowing which piece of silver to use for what dish, and knowing how to arrange it all."

"So how can I be sure these forks aren't meant to be here, then?" I teased as I pointed to a set of forks on the side of the plate. "Since you're technically the only one who knows where they go, how do we know you're not just making it up?"

He straightened up and folded his arms. "Well, you're going to have to trust me."

I turned toward the kitchen. "Trust Chase Anderson? Ha! I'd rather trust a—"

Chase clutched my elbow, stopping me. "Would you rather trust a knight?" His deep voice tickled my ear.

"A—a knight?" All of the sudden that weird feeling was back. My heart began to race.

"Could you ever learn to trust a knight?" He stepped close behind me and released his hold on my elbow, but I didn't move. I couldn't.

Why am I having such a hard time breathing? "Chase?"

"Always?"

Always. The echo of the word vibrated down to the small of my back and up again. My brain felt warm and I couldn't think properly. He took another step closer and rested his hands lightly on my shoulders. Hugo Boss tickled my senses. I knew if I didn't move away soon, I would be a massive pile of putty.

I did the only thing I could do in that moment. I called for my mother. "Mom, l–look at what Chase has done to the table." He stepped back.

My mom entered the room. "What, honey?"

I took a deep breath of air that smelled like Thanksgiving dinner instead of Chase. "Look at the table. What do you think?" I sputtered. I stepped farther away from the table and willed myself not to run into Chase's arms and beg to let me smell him again. His cologne suddenly had the wildest hold over my senses. Never before had I felt the need to be as far away as possible from something, while craving to be near it. I swear if I didn't know better, I'd say Hugo Boss was my kryptonite.

After dinner, we all went over to the Anderson home for dessert. Every year our families swapped who would host the dinner and who would host dessert. This year, the Andersons had invited a few other families, in addition to mine, to their place for dessert. I shouldn't have been, but I was surprised to see the Harts come in the door. And when a sheepish Taylor and Chloe followed shortly after, I really freaked!

"Taylor? Chloe? How long have you guys been in town? Why don't I ever know anything anymore?"

Chloe laughed and enveloped me in a warm hug. "We just got here this morning. We've been over at my parents' house, eating dinner."

Taylor had his hands full of pumpkin pies. "I would hug you too," he said, "but my—"

"Hands are a bit full," I finished for him as I took one of the pies. "There. Now you can one-arm hug me." I giggled when he squeezed my shoulders. I took the other pie and set them both on the sideboard.

All of a sudden, Chase yelled, "Taylor! Get over here and give me a hug."

"Thanks." Taylor smiled at me before he walked up to his brother.

Chase grabbed him and slapped him on the back in the typical guy-to-guy hug. "I see how it is. Go hang out with your girlfriend's family before you see me. I know how loved I really am." He reached up and ruffled Taylor's hair.

Laughing, Taylor ducked. "So how have you been? What's it like back in America? Are you missing Spain yet? Hey, Chloe, come here. You've gotta meet Chase."

"Oops, I've been summoned." She grinned. "Wanna join me?"

"Sure." I followed happily.

"Okay, Chase," Taylor said loud enough for anyone in the house to hear. "I know Chloe's really hot, but you've gotta promise me that you'll remember she's mine."

"Whatever!" Chloe rolled her eyes as Chase swooped her up in a bear hug.

Laughter bubbled out of her. "Um, thanks," she gasped as he set her down. "Now I know where Taylor learned how to give such energetic hugs."

Chase chuckled. "We both got them from our great-grandpa Darcy Taylor. That man could squeeze you to death."

"Well, at least you'd die happy." Taylor grinned over at me. "You met Grandpa Darcy before he died, didn't you?"

I smiled at the memory. "Yeah. He gave me a ton of candy bars. My mom almost lost her mind. I was only seven or eight." I turned to Chloe. "My mom is a stickler about kids and candy. Their grandpa drove her nuts when he was visiting that time."

"That's why he'd hug us so hard, so he could sneak it in our pockets when no one was looking," Taylor explained. "Like I said, you'd die happy."

"Grandpa Darcy's hugs were the best," Chase said.

"So where's my candy?" Chloe looked impishly at all of us. "I mean, come on, if I have to survive an Anderson hug, I should get something for it, right?"

Taylor laughed. "Want some pie?"

"Ha ha." She shook her head and headed toward the kitchen. "I'm going in to help your mom. Anybody else coming?"

"Sure," Taylor said. He turned to me as we walked through the archway leading to the back of the house. "Did Zack make it back this time?"

I shook my head. I'd figured Taylor would be sad when my stepbrother couldn't make it. "Nope. That's two Thanksgivings in a row. My stepdad was a bit depressed. But he'll be here for Christmas."

"Christmas is the best part! That's when your parents spoil you rotten anyway."

"Are you coming back for Christmas?"

Taylor looked ahead at Chloe, who was hugging his mom. "Actually, I'm hoping to surprise Chloe for Christmas. He wiggled his eyebrows, held out his left hand, and pointed to a ring on his finger.

SIXTEEN

♥

Excuse me, but I think I dropped
something—my jaw!

I whipped my head up to meet his blue eyes. "Are you . . . are you— Did you and Chloe—"

"What? No!" Taylor laughed out loud, causing a few heads to turn in our direction. He pulled me back into an alcove and quietly said, "It's a purity ring. Chloe got it for me on our anniversary in April. She has one too, but I'm hoping to update it."

"Purity ring?"

"Come on! Everyone knows what a purity ring is." I stared at him in confusion until he sighed and whispered, "It's a pledge not to, you know, do it, until you're married."

"Oh." *I'm such a dork.* My face turned bright red. Thank goodness Taylor had the decency to ignore it.

"Anyway, I want to get her something special. Something to let her know I mean business."

"Oh." *Ohhh!*

"Right now, I think our parents would freak if we announced an engagement, but I really want to."

Eeeh. "An engagement?"

"Not now!" Taylor said, hushing me. And then his face took on the happiest expression I'd ever seen. "But one day soon, yeah, that's the plan. I would love to ask Chloe to marry me."

"Well, for what it's worth. I think you're perfect for each other."

He laughed quietly. "I just can't believe she puts up with me. I swear I'm the luckiest guy on the planet."

His smile was so bright it almost blinded me.

"Hey, Taylor!" Chase hollered good-naturedly. "Stop hiding and help."

Taylor winked and was gone. For a moment I stood back from the group. Then I wandered into another room to think. It had been almost two years since Taylor had taken me to morp his senior year. Two years since he could no longer hide his crush on Chloe. At that dance, he couldn't take his eyes off her. And that was the night I pushed him out of my heart and let him go. Someone who looked at a girl the way he had looked at Chloe needed to feel guilt-free in pursuing her. Besides, I realized I wanted someone to stare at me like that.

My fingers trailed lightly over the Andersons' console table in the empty entertaining room. *What would it be like to have someone so in love with me that I'd feel safe and protected forever?* Chase was right. I used to have a little crush on Taylor—okay, so it was a huge crush. But looking back, I could see how much I was just bowled over with him being Taylor Anderson. I hadn't dug deeper to see who he really was. To me, he was just the guy every other girl was in love with, so it was easy for me to imagine myself in love with him, too.

I want to be in love. The idea stunned me for a moment and I froze, thinking it over. *I do! I want to have someone see me, the real me, and love me anyway.* With a groan, I sat down on the nearest sofa. *Why does everyone think I'm such a snob?* There was no way I was going to find the guy of my dreams if I couldn't attract him. *What guy, besides shallow losers like Elton, would want a girl he thought was conceited?* Which brought me to a much more contemplative thought—*Am I conceited?*

"Emmalee! There you are."

I turned my head and tried not to sigh when I saw Claire making her way toward me. *Can't a girl get any privacy?* "Hi, Claire—"

"I was wondering where you were! I've been trying to find you this whole—Wow! What a pretty fireplace! Can you believe the size of this house—we love this house! It always makes me so happy to come. Chloe is just so lucky. None of us could believe it when my big sister captured Taylor's heart. I mean *the* Taylor Anderson—tee he he! I giggled for three days straight when I heard they were going out! He's so nice too, don't you think so? Oh! Look at this couch! Wow, it's so comfortable! You have to try this one—oh, never mind I see yours and mine are the same—but aren't they so . . . Cassidy! Come in! You have to try these cushions out. See, sit here by me. Now aren't they . . . . this reminds me of when Ethan came over earlier. Doesn't it remind you of when he came over? He sat on our couch and we all talked about the coziness of the cushions. And he ate a lot for dinner! Emma, have you ever seen Ethan eat?" She stopped and looked up at me expectantly.

Oh, is it my turn to talk? "No, I haven't." And then before Claire could break in again, I added, "I'm sorry. Did you say Ethan Franklin was at your house for dinner today?"

"Yep!" She was all smiles. "Not only did we have Ethan, but we had all the Franklins over! Even Madison, Chloe's friend, was there and her dad, and then of course Taylor."

Ethan went to their house for Thanksgiving dinner? Good grief. The Harts had better guests than we did. "So, um—" *How to say this delicately . . .* "Why are you—" *Why are you here?* And then all at once I knew the answer, before Claire could confirm it. The Harts came because of Taylor. Even though they'd had a slew of guests for dinner, they'd obviously ended their evening early so they could come for dessert here.

{♥}

"Emma, can you help me clear off the rest of the plates?" My mother's look told me I wasn't allowed to say no.

I smiled. "Sure." Reaching around Mrs. Hart's arm, I collected her used plate while she chatted away with Chase's mom. Chloe's dad was quick to pass me his plate, along with Chloe's and Taylor's. "Thanks," I muttered. As I reached down to fetch another plate to add to the pile I was carrying, the dishes began to slip.

"Whoa!" Chase was at my side in an instant. "Here." He settled the plates in my arms. "You take those into your mom, and I'll follow you with the rest."

"Thanks."

My smile was wasted. He had already turned and begun collecting the rest of the Andersons' china. I wandered into the kitchen and gently set the dishes on the counter next to my mom. She had filled the sink with hot soapy water.

"And before you say anything, young lady, yes, we are going to wash all of these dishes ourselves. And no, the Andersons' maid is not here today. They gave her the day off to spend with her family."

Just my luck. "Did I say anything?" I asked innocently.

"You didn't have to. I know you well."

"So is there a reason we do this every time we're over here?" I complained as I scraped remnants of pie into the middle sink, which had a garbage disposal. "I never see the Andersons help us with our dishes."

My mother gave me "the look" and took the first few plates from my hands. As she rinsed them, she reminded me, "No matter how many blessings you have been accustomed to, I hope you will always remember the times before I married Adrian Bradford, and you were just Emmalee Glumm. We didn't have a dishwasher or anything. To wash someone's dishes is a sign of respect. It's a way of saying thank you. And no matter what—whether they return the favor or not—we love our friends and will wash their dishes for them." She dunked a plate into the soapy water and cleaned it with the sponge she held in her gloved hands.

My mom and I both jumped when Chase said from very close by, "Here are the rest of the plates. If you'll scoot over, Em, I'll set them down right next to you."

My face flamed and I wondered if he had heard my ungracious comments. I couldn't gauge anything from his face, because he kept his head turned toward my mom.

"Thank you, Chase." She smiled up at him. "You are so nice."

"No problem." He shrugged and turned to me. "Need help drying?"

"Uh, sure."

"Great." He did a full circle around the kitchen, then sheepishly asked, "Do you know where the dish towels are? I think I know your kitchen better than my own."

My mom laughed. "Third drawer down on your right."

"Where?"

"Here." I walked over to the towel drawer and handed him one. "You do know how to dry dishes, don't you?" I raised an eyebrow.

"I did work for the toughest restaurant manager in all of New Mexico, remember?" Chase flipped his towel expertly in the air and rested it on his shoulder.

"I thought you couldn't hand-dry dishes in restaurants."

"Dang. You know that?" He grinned at me.

I laughed. "Are you ready for your first lesson?" I leaned over and collected one of the clean plates in the growing pile on the counter. Just as I was about to dry it, my cell rang. "Oops! Hang on." I handed the plate to Chase and fumbled to pull the phone out of my pocket.

"Hello?"

"Hey, Emma. This is Ethan Franklin."

"Ethan?" *Oh my gosh! He called me! Eeeh.* I beamed up at Chase and then over at my mom. Neither looked overly thrilled when I said his name. "Uh, hang on." I switched the phone to my other ear and walked over to the back of the kitchen by the Andersons' breakfast table. "What's up?"

"It's all set for us to go to the movie tomorrow afternoon. There's a whole group of us going. You want to come?"

"Sure! That'd be awesome. I'd love to go to a movie." I glanced up at my mom and she jerked her head slightly in Chase's direction. Thank goodness his back was to me. *Fine.* "Can Chase come too?" I asked.

At the mention of his name, he looked over at me. I smiled and listened as Ethan said, "Okay, that'll be great. He's cool. And hey, you promise you'll sit next to me, right?"

"Sit next to you?" I giggled. "What if I don't want to sit next to you?"

"Oh, you will. I promise." Ethan's whisper tickled my ear.

"So, is it a date then?" I asked teasingly, lowering my voice. "I mean, I think you can only claim a seat next to me if you're paying my way."

A utensil clattered loudly on the floor. I glanced up to see Chase bend down behind the counter to pick it up.

"Why else do you think I'd go to the trouble of getting a group together, if it wasn't to ask you out? Of course it's a date."

I giggled again. "You went to all this trouble just for me?"

Chase interrupted from across the room. "What time are we supposed to be there?"

"Oh, Chase wants to know when we need to be there."

"And tell him I'll be taking you," Chase added. "There's no reason for him to come out here and pick you up if I'm going too."

Good grief! "Ethan? Chase says he'll give me a ride to the movie, too."

"Are you kidding me?" Ethan laughed. "What if I wanted to pick you up?"

"Then you'll live and settle for buying me popcorn."

"And Milk Duds?" he joked.

"Hmm. How about you get me Junior Mints and we'll call it good."

"So, I buy you movie tickets, I buy you popcorn, *and* I buy you Junior Mints, but I can't pick you up and drive you home?"

"Nope."

Ethan groaned. "That's a tough break for a guy, you know?"

"Why?" I didn't think my grin could get any bigger.

"Don't you know?" his voice got a bit deeper. "It's the only time a guy can really get to know a girl. Outside on her front porch as he kiss—"

"So, what time are we meeting?" Chase interrupted again.

Can't the guy see I'm on the phone? Argh. Speaking of timing, he has the worst.

SEVENTEEN

♥

Hey, baby, what's your sign?

The group movie thing actually went pretty well. Much better than I thought it would, considering all the train-wreck possibilities, especially once I realized the Franklin brothers had invited not only Elton and his new girlfriend, but the Hart sisters as well.

Cassidy, fine. I can understand why as Chloe's sister she would need to be included, but to invite Claire—the youngest one—too? Was there no escaping the girl?

By the time I'd gotten off the phone with Ethan the night before, Chase had arranged to invite and pick up Hannah, too. Which was really cool until I remembered, as I held the car door open for her to get out, that I'd forgotten to tell her that Ethan had invited Elton and his new girlfriend.

I looked up to see Claire bounding toward us through the parking lot, and suddenly she didn't seem so daunting after all. I tried to shield Hannah from seeing Elton's sleek sports car glide into a parking spot a few feet from us, but I was too late.

"You've got to be kidding me. He's here too? This is so embarrassing!" She moaned behind me.

I turned around and placed my hands on her shoulders. "Don't worry about it. Stand up tall, slap on your biggest smile, and congratulate them."

"What? No way! There is no way I'm going near that guy." Hannah started to climb back in the car.

"Hannah, wait."

"Look, you go on without me. I don't feel so good anyway. I think I'll take a nap."

"What? In Chase's car?" I didn't think she'd take it *that* hard. I wondered if I should just take her home and forget about the movie. After all, friends come first. "Hannah—"

In a flash Chase was next to me. "Hannah, do you mind sitting with me in the theater?" he asked in a tone I'd never heard him use before.

She looked past me, her mouth hanging open. "Shut up! Are you trippin' me?"

He flashed a killer smile. "No. I'd like to buy your ticket, too, if you don't mind."

Hannah smiled up at him, obviously in a daze, before she blinked and nodded her head. "Uh, sure."

"Great!" His grin lit up his tanned features nicely, if I did say so myself. He held his hand out for her, and I was pleased to see the huge smile break out on her face.

Chase Anderson is the nicest guy ever! What a sweetheart! I was so impressed I was practically giddy.

"Thanks!" I whispered and smiled up at him as he passed me, still holding Hannah's hand.

His answering grunt left much to be desired, but I giggled anyway. By the time I had followed them a few steps, Claire had reached us, and Elton and his girlfriend waited by their car.

"Hey, guys! Can you believe we're going to a movie!" Claire said loudly. "I love movies, especially scary ones. I hope this movie is scary! Does anyone know what movie we're going to see? It's been so long since I've seen one, I don't even know what's out. So what's out? What are we gonna watch? Ooh! I hope it's something really scary—well, not too scary. I can't watch rated-R movies. You guys know that, right? I mean, you know that me and Cassidy and Chloe don't watch any really bad movies. I just like the sorta scary ones. Oh, Cass! Look who's here! Chase came with Hannah and Emmalee! Aren't you excited? She—"

"So is the movie out here now, or what?" Elton called to us from his car.

Chase muttered something under his breath. Pulling Hannah with him, he walked toward the theater, passing Elton without saying a word. By the time Claire and I made it to Elton and his girlfriend, we'd been joined by Cassidy, Chloe, and Taylor, which I was totally grateful for, because it helped take the awkwardness out of meeting Ashley Templeton alone.

"I don't think I've seen you around Farmington, have I?" I asked, trying to be friendly to Elton's girlfriend, but wanting to be anywhere else.

She flipped her stylishly fringed hair to one shoulder and looked me up and down. "Oh, you would know if you've seen me," she said smugly. "Everyone knows me at Pedra Vista. Let's just say I'm something like the crowned queen over there."

"Oh." *Full of ourselves, aren't we?* "So do you like Pedra Vista?" I asked. About ten years before, the city had split the main high school into two. Pedra Vista was definitely our rival school. Elton Bloomfield *would* pick a girl from there. No one from our school would be able to stand the jerk!

Ashley ignored my question. "You're Emmalee Bradford, aren't you?" She looked coyly at Elton.

Great. I wonder if he's said something to her. Nah, probably not. He's too much of a coward. "Yep. I'm Emma."

She smiled, showing all of her teeth. It was probably her attempt at my Bradford smile. "I've heard a lot about you."

"You have?" *Maybe Elton did say something.* I glanced up at him, but he was talking to Taylor and Chloe.

"Yep." Ashley linked her arm through mine and began to walk with me across the parking lot to the movie theater. "I think you and I are really going to get along."

I was shocked but not impressed. "You do, huh?"

"Yep!" We stepped up on the curb as she continued, "You and I have so much in common, it's like we were destined to be friends."

Destined to be friends? O-kay. Somebody is seriously delusional. "So, how did you hear about me?" I asked just for curiosity's sake.

"Oh, everyone knows about you! I mean, you're Emmalee Bradford. So tell me. Just between you and me, was that Chase Anderson? And is he taken or single?"

"Chase?" I stopped walking.

"Shhh!" She giggled and pulled me toward the door. "Don't say it so loud. Elton will hear you."

"You like Chase?" I asked quietly.

"Well, duh! I mean, the obvious choice is Taylor, of course." She turned to look behind her as we walked through the door, I assume to drool over Taylor. "But hello, it's clear he's taken. Which won't be for long if I have any say in the matter, believe me. If Taylor thinks he's found the girl of his dreams, he hasn't met me yet."

I stared at her. *Is she for real?*

She allowed the door to swing close, and it almost hit me as I made my way in.

"Well, that was until I caught a glimpse of Chase just now," she said. "That was Chase, wasn't it—the guy who came storming past Elton and me? Surely you can see the family resemblance. He didn't look too happy to be with that girl—what's her name?"

"You mean Hannah Smith?"

Ashley nodded and drew me closer to whisper, "Figures. I should've known her name would be Hannah." She sighed. "No one really can compete with the name Ashley. There's just a certain ring to it, don't you think?"

I think I have a headache.

"At least that's what all my friends have told me." She smiled and flipped her hair again. "Ashley Templeton. Yep, remember that name. It's going places." As she caught sight of Chase, she released my arm and sauntered over to grace him with her presence.

Yeah, your name's goin' places, all right. Right back to the juvenile detention center you came from. The hussy. Who does she think she is, trying to weasel her way into the Anderson family?

"Emma! You're here!"

I turned to see Ethan jog up to me with a couple of tickets in his hand. "I just got the tickets. When did you get here?"

"A few minutes ago. Were you able to get in to the movie we were hoping for?"

"Yep! It was released today. I've got the rest of the group tix on reserve. But they better get in quick, cuz they won't hold 'em much longer." He scanned the foyer and then looked out the floor-to-ceiling windows that lined the front of the theater. "Oh, here they are. Great! They're just walking in." He waved and then said, "Just a sec. I'll be right back."

I looked back to see Chase gently disengaging himself from Elton's leech, Ashley. Chase still had a firm grip on Hannah's hand, which I found promising. I chuckled wickedly to myself. *Maybe Ashley will get the hint and go away.*

"So what's she like?"

Chloe's voice near my elbow startled me, but I recovered quickly. "Who?"

"Elton's new girl. Is she nice?"

Nice? About as nice as a viper. "Uh, Ashley's okay."

Chloe smothered a giggle and raised her brow. "That bad, huh? Chase told Taylor how he had to keep you from decking Elton."

Chase talks too much. "He did, huh?"

"Yep. Kind of surprising he bounced back so quickly, don't you think?"

I snorted. "Bounced back from what? There was nothing for the guy to bounce back from, believe me."

"You think so?" Chloe grinned slowly as she looked over to where Elton and the other guys stood in line. "Rumor has it he'd been in love with you for something like two years."

Don't remind me. "Really?"

Chloe took a step toward the concession stand. "That's just what I've heard. Do you wanna come with me to get some popcorn?"

"Sure. But won't Taylor be mad? I mean, won't he insist on buying it?"

She laughed. "Probably. But when have I ever worried about what would make him mad?" She moved her curly red hair off her shoulder. "He knows me too well now to be surprised at anything I do. Besides, if I don't get the treats, how am I going to get the ones I want?"

"You have a point. Guys never get it, do they?"

"Nope. I mean, honestly, how hard is it to decipher when a girl wants Red Vines or Whoppers? And yet he still can't figure it out."

I shook my head as we approached the counter. "Yeah, but do you ever know what you want before coming up to the counter?"

"No. But don't you tell Taylor that."

I laughed. I really liked Chloe. She was so perfect for Taylor. I wished I had taken the time to get to know her more in high school.

"Chloe!" The shrill scream from Madison rang out through the whole lobby. Everyone turned to watch the tall girl run up to us and squeeze Chloe.

I looked over to where Carson and Ethan were talking. From a distance, it was obvious how rugged and outdoorsy they were, compared to the other male specimens in line. The Franklin boys' aura was just naturally cool. In fact, standing next to Elton, they put the poor guy to shame. *I bet he wishes he had half their confidence. In fact, he probably wishes his big toe had half their confidence!*

"Who is that girl circling around my guy?" Madison nearly growled.

I had to stop myself from laughing out loud. "Let me introduce you to Ashley Templeton. Apparently she believes she is every man's dream. And even though she's taken by Elton Bloomfield over there, she's still on the prowl."

Chloe laughed. "I'll say! That, my friends, is a girl who obviously has a thing for outdoorsy animal magnetism. Can she seriously get any closer to poor Carson?"

"Well, she better get her prowling butt back to her own boyfriend," Madison said, "or she's gonna see some *serious* animal magnetism. And I don't think her pretty nose is going to like it."

Poor Ashley didn't quite fit in. I would've felt sorry for her if I didn't think it was so darn funny.

EIGHTEEN

♥

I have an owie on my lip.
Will you kiss it and make it better?

About halfway through the movie, Ethan's hands collided with mine in the huge bag of popcorn we shared. It should've totally made my heart race. I waited for a small pitter-patter or something, but nothing happened. I was beginning to wonder if I was just meant to find love for everyone else and be completely immune to it myself. *Maybe I'll never marry. I'll be, like, some old lady who sits around knitting and never actually leaves her house. Okay, that was a scary thought.* It was scary enough for me to take matters into my own hands. Literally. I waited a few more minutes before resting my hand in the bag. It didn't take long until Ethan's hand bumped into mine again. This time, I laced my fingers through his and pretended they were caught.

"Oh, I'm sorry," I whispered.

Chuckling, he lifted our joined hands out of the bag and flipped his around so his fingers were cradling mine. "There. Much better."

Shocked at how easy that was, I looked up at him. He winked. *Yes!* My heart melted and I smiled at him. *He really is hot.* We held hands for the rest of the show.

Afterward, he insisted on taking me home. Chase didn't complain much, though I could tell he thought Ethan was being impractical. But hey, what girl doesn't like a guy to be impractical for her every now and then?

At my front door, Ethan hemmed and hawed a bit while he waited for me to go inside. I didn't want to. I was completely curious to see what his kiss would be like. So I waited. It was cold. I'm not a huge fan of the cold, so after a few more minutes, I finally sighed and said, "Are you gonna kiss me, or what?"

Ethan's burst of laughter made me giggle. "You're, uh, not shy, are you?" he asked, grinning down at me.

"Me? Shy? I think I can safely say the answer to that question is no." I smiled my Bradford smile and Ethan took a step back, his eyes never leaving my mouth. *Man, I love this smile,* I thought, stepping forward. "Are you trying to tell me that you don't want to kiss me goodnight?" I asked, lowering my voice. Another step brought me within a foot of Ethan's shoes.

"I, uh, no. I'm not saying that." His green eyes flashed under the porch light a moment before he lowered his gaze. His lashes rested against his cheeks for a moment, and then those eyes pierced mine. "I—I can't."

Huh? "You can't? You can't kiss me?"

"No."

"Why?" I blurted before I could stop myself.

Ethan's eyes searched mine a moment and the corner of his mouth lifted in a lopsided grin. "Good night, Emmalee Bradford." He took a step forward and kissed me gently on the cheek, his slightly stubbly chin brushing my jaw. "I'll see you tomorrow morning," he whispered in my ear.

"Okay." I smiled. "I'll be up bright and early. Thanks." During the movie, he'd asked me to breakfast, and I was excited.

"Bye." Ethan gave a short salute with his hand and then was gone.

I walked quietly into the house and locked the door. After I said good night to my mom and stepdad, I walked into my room, turned on the light, and gasped. There on my bed was Clementine, snoring softly on a large satin pillow. She had a bright red bow around her collar. And under her paws was a note. I set my purse on my desk next to my laptop and carefully removed the white paper.

Dear Em,

Clem's finally eight weeks old. I hope you love her as much as we do.

She's a real sweetheart. I had my mom bring her over while we were out to surprise you. So, surprise!

Love,
Chase

Aww! I knelt and softly rubbed the bridge of the puppy's fuzzy nose. "You are the most cutest puppy in the whole world." I rested my head next to hers on the pillow. "And I needed you today. How Chase knew I would need you, I have no idea, but wow, you are welcome!"

Clementine opened one black eye and focused on me a moment before bringing her head up and opening her other eye. With a happy yap she was on all fours in an instant. I may not have gotten the kiss I wanted out of Ethan, but little Clementine sure made up for it. I was bestowed with sloppy puppy kisses all over my eyes, cheeks, and chin as I scooped her in my arms and sat down on the bed. Her tiny tail thumped happily against my hand and I chuckled.

"If you're this happy to see me when I come home every day, I won't need a silly boy to fall in love with anyway." I crinkled her bow with my chin as I tucked her further into the crook of my neck. "I'll just keep you forever. How does that sound?"

Clementine gave one more tiny yap before burrowing farther into my shoulder and licking my neck.

I chuckled. "I love you too!"

About twenty minutes later, just as I was tucking her into her little doggy bed on the floor next to my bed, my cell rang. I wondered who would call so late.

"Hello?"

"Hey, Em. It's Chase."

"Oh, hi."

"Just calling to see if you got Clem all right."

I grinned and plopped onto my comforter. "Yeah, she's asleep next to me. Thanks! She was an awesome surprise."

"I'm glad you're happy. And hey, is it okay if Georgia and I come over tomorrow? She wanted to visit you and Clem."

"Sure. Oh, make sure you come in the afternoon. Ethan's taking me to breakfast in the morning."

"Really? *You?* He's taking *you* to breakfast?"

Is it that hard to believe? "Um, yeah." I rolled my eyes. It was too bad Chase couldn't see the effect. "He had a great time with me tonight and wanted to see me again."

"Are you sure about that?"

I snorted into the phone. "Are you really asking me if I can tell whether a guy is interested in me or not? As if I wouldn't know. To answer your question, yes, I'm sure he had a good time."

"I'm sure he had a good time too, just not with the girl you're thinking."

I sat up. "What is that supposed to mean?" I was beginning to get irritated.

"Haven't you seen the way he looks at Cassidy when you're not around?"

"Cassidy? As in Cassidy Hart? There is no way Ethan Franklin has even looked twice at that girl. Why would he? She's so quiet, anyway. Besides, if he likes her, why would he even think about asking me out? Seriously, Chase, you were not meant to be a matchmaker, so don't quit your day job, okay?"

He was quiet so long I wondered if he was still on the phone with me. Finally, he let out a weary sigh. "Em, do me a favor and promise me you won't fall for the guy, okay?"

"Why?"

"Just promise me."

"Look, I'm not in love with him, if that's what you mean."

"Good."

"But I'm not going to stop something if it happens."

"Did he kiss you tonight?"

"Chase, what is going on? Why do you care?"

"Did he kiss you?"

"I'm not going to tell you that!"

"Em?"

"No, okay? Are you happy now? He did not kiss me. Unless you call that peck he gave my cheek a kiss."

"Hey, don't get mad. Someone has to watch out for you now that Zack is gone."

I fell back into my pillows. "Is that what this is all about— you trying to be my older brother?" *Sheesh.* "Chase, I'm a big girl now. I don't need an older brother."

"So you keep saying, but I haven't seen you prove that yet."

"Now I've got to prove that I'm mature? You're like three years older than me. Anything I do is going to seem immature."

"Look, Em. There's something about that guy that's just not right. So sue me if I happen to be worried about you."

"Once and for all, there is nothing wrong with Ethan Franklin!" I practically shouted into the phone. *When will Chase ever let up?*

"Shh! You don't want to wake your whole house, do you?"

Grrr. "Why don't you like him, anyway?" I asked in a much quieter voice. "Has he done anything to you? Huh?"

"No. He just seems like he's hiding something, that's all."

Now I really wished Chase could see my rolling eyes. "Hiding something?"

"Until I know what it is, I want you to be a bit leery of the guy."

I took a deep breath. "Anything else you wanted to add, Detective Anderson?"

"For a girl who thinks she knows a lot about relationships and the people around her," Chase said in a deeper tone, "you're sure missing a rather large chunk of the picture."

What in the—? "What is that supposed to mean?"

"You're the expert on love. You figure it out."

I jolted when the phone went dead in my ear.

Figure what out? Ugh. Why does Chase always talk in riddles? Can't he just say what he means for once and be done with it?

I leaned over and turned off my lamp before I crawled under the covers. In the dark, I closed my eyes and willed myself not to think about Chase's stupid comments and warnings. Instead, I tried to focus on the perfect outfit to wow Ethan with the next day. But Chase's words kept coming back into my mind. Why did he have to ruin everything? Now I'd look all suspiciously at Ethan the whole time I was with him. I punched my pillow and rolled over. *Urk! If I lose sleep over this, I'm going to be ticked. And I know a certain dark-haired, blue-eyed guy that'll definitely hear about it!*

The next morning when Ethan came to my door, I was surprised to see Cassidy and her little sister sitting in his Jeep in the driveway.

So much for my outfit.

"Hey," Ethan leaned over and whispered, "sorry about bringing them along. Last night Carson opened his big mouth and practically invited Taylor and Chloe to hang with us. Well, Chloe's sisters were in the room right there, so Taylor invited them, too."

"No problem. The more the merrier, right?" *See? Ethan does like me, Chase.*

Ethan wrapped his arm around me as we descended the porch steps. "I knew you'd understand. You're awesome, Emma. You know that, right?"

I smiled flirtatiously up at him. "Know that I'm awesome? Of course I do. Who else would put up with you?"

He halted a moment and then laughed out loud. "You know, I think I really do like you. There's something great about a girl who can pack a punch."

"So you like someone who gives as good as she gets?"

"Or better." He chuckled. As we approached the Jeep he whispered, "It's definitely much nicer to have a girl who actually talks." And then with a glance at Claire through the window, he quickly added, "Talks intelligently."

As he ushered me into the front passenger seat and shut the door, I decided I was pretty impressed that he found me intelligent and worth listening to. I mean, what girl wouldn't get her head turned by something like that? *Today is going to be amazing. I just know it.*

"Hello, Emmalee! We're so excited you're coming too! Aren't we, Cass? Do you know where we're going for breakfast? I like your outfit by the way—it's cute! Ethan said it was a secret where we're going, but I thought maybe he told you. Oh! You didn't tell her? Oh! So it's a surprise for you too, then? Well, isn't this going to be fun?"

On second thought, I don't think today is going to be that amazing after all.

NINETEEN

♥

Can I take a picture of you? I want Santa Claus to know exactly what to get me for Christmas.

"What? Someone bought you a brand-new camera—worth like a thousand dollars—and you don't know who it was?" I blurted out to Cassidy over the restaurant table while Ethan and Claire were filling our drinks. "Are you kidding me?"

I guess I'd spoken a little louder than I should've, because Cassidy turned beet red and ducked her head.

"But don't you have an idea who it might be?" I asked, lowering my voice. "I mean, my parents have never spent that much on a camera for me. You must know who it is."

Smiling vaguely, she looked at me and said, "No." She sipped her ice water, then suddenly set the glass down. "I wish I did know, really. I mean, I would like to thank them, you know?"

I snorted. "Thank them? I think I'd be kissing the person who gave me a gift like that!"

Cassidy smiled uneasily and glanced around the room. Clearly, she wasn't comfortable with the idea of kissing whoever her benefactor was.

This is a mystery! I thought excitedly. *Who could it be?*

"What put that expression on your face?" Ethan asked me as he set my juice on the table.

I glanced up at Cassidy. She was smiling at Claire as she approached, chattering nonstop over the many different juices. I leaned over and whispered, "Someone secretly bought Cassidy a high-end camera and left it at her house last night. It was there when she came home from the movie."

"W–wow!" Ethan almost choked on his juice. "Are you kidding me?"

"No," I whispered and caught a faint flush rise to Cassidy cheeks again. "Who in the world do you think would do that? Does she have a boyfriend?"

"I don't kno–ow." Ethan wiggled his eyebrows at me. And then he asked loud enough to be heard across the table, "Should we ask her?"

"No!" I waved my hand to shush him. "Will you behave?"

"Why?" he asked, then added quietly, "I think it's a mystery that needs to be solved, don't you?" He glanced over at Cassidy, who quickly turned her head away.

Great. She can *hear us. Ugh.* When I caught Ethan's eye again, I saw that he was fully aware of the fact too. And he liked it! *The punk.*

"Will you knock it off? You're embarrassing her!" I said.

"You know who I think it was?"

I leaned in. "Who?"

"Come on! You can't guess?"

I grinned and shook my head.

He matched my grin and whispered near my ear, "Taylor Anderson."

No way! I pulled back to look Ethan in his way-too-flirtatious eyes.

Ethan grabbed my hand and pulled me toward him. "Think about it. It's perfect. Who else would know Cassidy as well as he does? Besides, he's totally got the dough to blow on something like that without even blinking."

"But why?" I whispered in his ear. "He has Chloe."

I felt Ethan's hand clutch my other one. "But what if Taylor secretly likes Cassidy?"

"Yeah, right!"

"Wasn't it Taylor who first tipped off Chloe when that Blake guy was going after Cassidy?"

"Yeah, but—" I gasped. "No, way! You really think so?"

Ethan moved back a little. "Well, I figure the only other person it could be is Chase."

Chase? "Nope. I think you're right. It's definitely Taylor. It makes perfect sense." I decided to ignore the memory of him smiling when he told me about Chloe's Christmas present. It had to be Taylor. There was no way I was even going to think about Chase falling for Cassidy.

Ethan let go of my left hand and downed the rest of his juice in a quick gulp. "Okay, here's the deal. I'm gonna walk over and refill my glass. When I come back, I'll walk up to Cassidy and say the name Taylor Anderson. You tell me if she blushes, okay?"

I smiled and yanked my other hand away. "No, you can't."

"Watch me." Ethan smirked.

"Ethan," I yelped as his chair scraped across the tile when he stood. "You're incorrigible."

He grinned wickedly at me and winked. "I know."

Once he made it over to the juice dispensers, I felt brave enough to take a peek in Cassidy's direction. She had twirled her napkin so tightly around her finger that the tip of the appendage had gone purple. Claire was still talking nonstop, but neither of us had a problem zoning her out. At least, Cassidy *pretended* to be listening to her little sister, but I knew better. She couldn't have been more aware of Ethan's and my behavior if a bright spotlight had descended over our heads and a whole slew of flame-throwing hula girls danced behind us. *Dang.*

Frantically, I watched Ethan beam as he approached our table, juice in hand. With another quick wink at me, he bent over Cassidy and whispered in her ear. She did blush. Worse than that, she refused to look at me. Actually, she was looking everywhere other than where I was sitting. As Ethan sauntered over to our side of the table, I had a sneaking suspicion he'd said more than the name Taylor Anderson. Just as I was getting ready to ask him about it, Taylor and Chloe arrived, with Madison and Carson close behind.

"Speak of the devil." Ethan chuckled as he sat down next to me again. He nodded in Cassidy's direction.

She quickly turned her head away as Chloe approached the table and flashed her pretty smile at us.

"Ethan! Emmalee! How are you guys?"

"What took you so long?" Claire asked her oldest sister.

"Sorry, guys, it was my fault." Madison laughed as she dodged Carson's hand. "I forgot to set my alarm. I was still asleep when they came to pick me up."

"Yep." He determinedly wrapped his arm around her waist. "Just like Sleeping Beauty."

"So did you kiss her and wake her up?" Ethan teased his brother.

"Yeah, right!" Madison laughed again and patted Carson's arm. "He's not that brave. He knows if he ever stepped a foot into my room, I'd kill him!"

"If your dad doesn't get to him first." Chloe giggled.

"Yeah, sometimes I'm a whole lot smarter than I look, little bro," Carson said.

Ethan threw his head back and laughed. "You left yourself wide open with that remark! There is so much I could throw back at you right now, but—"

"But you're gonna be nice instead?" Taylor offered before he turned toward Cassidy and said, "Hi, Cass."

"Hi." It looked like she wished she could die right then and there.

Taylor frowned at her for a moment, then walked over and sat down on the other side of Claire. Chloe followed and asked, "Hey, Claire. So what did you order?"

As I took another swallow of my juice, Ethan leaned in close to me again. "I bet that's why Taylor mentioned this date to Cass and Claire. He wanted me to invite them without it looking suspicious."

I nearly spit the juice across the table. *How cow!* Ethan's logic was making more and more sense the longer I considered it. "You think so?" I looked into his charming emerald eyes. Mischief danced in them, and I could tell he knew something that he wasn't saying. "What?" I grinned up at him. "Why are you looking at me like that?"

His expression transformed into complete innocence. "Looking like what? I'm not looking like anything."

I chewed on my lower lip while I studied his eyes.

Ethan widened them and moved closer. I almost smacked him away—he was slightly too close for comfort—but just then I caught a spark in his eyes again. "You know something. Out with it," I demanded.

For a moment, panic registered across his face, but quickly masked it with feigned surprise. "What, moi?" He chuckled. "What could I possibly know? I don't even live here, remember?"

"Don't give me that! Come on. What is it? There's something you want to hide, I can tell."

Ethan shook his head before tapping mine. "It's all in your head, blondie," he said and moved even closer toward me.

I swallowed and tried not to focus on his lips. "How do you expect me to believe that?"

"Trust me."

"Trust you?" Instantly, Chase's warning from the night before came rushing back to me. "What do you mean?"

Ethan studied my face. "Emma?"

"Yeah?" I whispered, completely unaware of anyone else around us.

"Can I—can I tell you something?"

"What?"

"Will you promise not to—"

Cassidy's glass dropped onto the table, and orange juice splattered everywhere.

"Oh my gosh!" she gasped. "I'm so sorry! Did that get on anyone? Please tell me my juice didn't spill on anyone. I'm such a klutz."

Taylor was next to her and mopping up the mess before she'd even finished talking. Ethan grabbed his napkin and mine and quickly slopped up the excess juice heading toward us. I saved what I could of the silverware and menus, but it was Taylor's murmured words to a mortified Cass that caused me to pause and look at Ethan.

"Don't worry, everything's fine," Taylor said. "We all spill our drinks sometimes. It's no big deal. Now come on and smile again. You have the prettiest smile I've ever seen—now let's see it."

The Anderson charm seemed to work on Cassidy. Ducking her head, she gave a little smile. Taylor tilted her chin up with his finger until she returned his gaze. Then Cassidy really smiled. Taylor was right. It was a very pretty smile.

I heard a ragged intake of breath next to me and realized Ethan must've caught the smile too. *Man, who knew Cassidy Hart could actually rival the Bradford smile?*

"Thanks for breakfast. It was, um, very enlightening." I smiled at Ethan as he walked me up the steps to my house.

"Yes, it was." He seemed to be in the same pensive mood he'd been in since Cassidy spilled her drink at the restaurant.

I tried to shake him from it. "So do you have any plans for today?"

"Plans?" He looked over as we approached the door. He stared at me a moment and then seemed to check himself. "Yeah, actually, I'm helping Carson on a couple of four-wheeling tours he's got booked this afternoon. I, uh, I would invite you along, but—"

I laughed. "You're not brave enough to face my mom?"

"Something like that." Ethan grinned. I was happy to see it was a much more normal grin this time. "So what are your plans?"

"My day is going to be fabulous! I've got Georgia, Chase's little sister, coming over to play with my new puppy."

"Your new puppy?"

"Yep." I held my hands behind my back and swayed back and forth. "Cassidy's not the only one who got a surprise present yesterday. Chase had li'l Clementine brought over for me while we were at the movie."

"Wow." Ethan rocked backwards, imitating my pose with his hands behind him. "It seems like the Anderson boys were full of surprises last night. First Cass and now you. I have to wonder what sort of claim they're trying to stake."

I couldn't help it, I burst out laughing. "Claim? You think Chase is staking a claim? On me? You couldn't be farther from the truth! That poor guy can't even stand me most of the time. Besides, I've been promised a puppy since before I knew he'd returned home. I'm sure he was just getting the little rascal out of his house so he didn't have to take care of it for me anymore." My giggles died abruptly when I saw the look on Ethan's face. "What? What is it?"

He walked toward me so quickly I instinctively took two steps back before I bumped into the front door. He followed. "Ethan?" I gulped, not sure what to make of the gleam I saw in his eyes.

"Is there something wrong with Chase being interested in you?" he asked slowly and distinctly.

"I, uh . . ." I trailed off lamely. *No.*

Ethan took another step closer. "Do you believe it's impossible for a guy to be attracted to you, then? Even an older guy?"

What is he saying? He is two years older than me . . . All of a sudden my throat went dry.

He softly brushed a few tendrils of hair off my brow. "You're a very beautiful girl, Emmalee Bradford."

"I—I am?" *For Pete's sake! Can I act like a bigger loser? Of course, I know I'm beautiful. Now it sounds like I'm fishing.* I winced and closed my eyes so I wouldn't have to see Ethan smile at the blush I could feel rising to my cheeks.

I felt his warmth as he moved in closer, his breath on my lips. My eyes flew open. His mouth was only millimeters from mine. *Oh my gosh! Is he going to kiss me?*

"Emma, stop me, please," he whispered. "I don't know what's happened to me. But I can't—I can't kiss you. Please."

I had heard enough. With a shove to his chest, I sent him backwards. If I would've thought about it, I may have stayed long enough to hear his reasoning, but I didn't. Instead, I barged through my front door and slammed it shut behind me. *The nerve! Urgh! What moron puts a girl through that psychological meltdown without kissing her?* With a disgusted sigh, I stomped up the stairs to my room and to Clementine, determined to forget all about the very annoying Ethan Franklin.

TWENTY

♥

How was heaven when you left?

It didn't help that Chase and Georgia were super cute and friendly later that afternoon when they came to visit the puppy. For some reason, I just wasn't in the mood to be entertained by them. It took every bit of effort I had to be charming back, and even that attempt failed.

"You're a grumpy grouch today," Chase observed as he handed Clementine back to Georgia. They were both sitting on the floor of my bedroom. "What happened to make you all ornery?"

"Ornery?" I arched a brow and sat up on the bed. "Like I'm some old grandpa? That's the best adjective you could come up with?"

Chase raised his hands in mock surrender and leaned his back against the wall. "Hey, I just call it like I see it." He had the gall to chuckle at my expression.

The dork.

"So what happened?" he persisted.

Everything. "Nothing," I tucked my feet underneath me. "Why are you so positive something happened? Can't I have a bad day, just like everyone else?"

Chase searched my face for a moment and then watched Georgia ruffle Clem's ears. I thought I might be lucky and he'd drop the subject, but as usual, I wasn't lucky. His blue eyes practically pierced me with their intensity when he looked back up. "No. You don't have bad days."

I smirked back at him until I realized he was serious. "Come on, Chase, I have bad days just like everyone else. You know? Waking up on the wrong side of the bed—"

"Not without a reason." He brought his knee up and wrapped his arms around it. "Are you trying to tell me you had a bad dream last night?"

"No."

"Then something happened on your date."

Yeah, your brother started hitting on Cassidy, and Ethan's a— "Nothing happened."

"You're sure Ethan didn't try anything? He didn't kiss you, did he?"

"Ugh!" I threw a pillow at Chase and he caught it with one hand. "What is it with you and your paranoia about Ethan kissing me? Give me a break, okay? He didn't kiss me. He wouldn't kiss me. He doesn't want to kiss me! You got that? I'm sure no matter how many dates the guy takes me on, it'll still be the same. So stop worrying. For some reason, I'm some random freak of nature to the guy, anyway. He got like a centimeter away from my mouth and then panicked and totally begged for me to shove him away. Imagine that—the first guy, ever, who doesn't want to maul me. You should be praising the guy for his ability to withstand being tempted by me!"

I threw the other pillow at Chase for good measure. He caught that one too, then just stared at me.

Good. I've acted like such a weirdo I've made him speechless.

"Emma?" Georgia's voice snapped me out of my tirade.

Great. I forgot she was here. I tried to make my voice sound calm, but it came out strained and forced. "What, sweetie?"

"Don't be so sad cuz that boy didn't wanna kiss ya. I bet lots of other boys'll want to."

"Uh—" I was floored. Talk about feeling like an idiot. *I can't believe I lost it in front of her.* "Georgia, don't worry—"

"Huh, Chase? Lots of boys'll wanna kiss her, huh?"

His gaze flew to mine. "Yeah, I'm sure."

"Even you wanna kiss her, don't ya?" Georgia blinked innocently up at her older brother.

Ack! I wished I could crawl into a hole, and I could see I wasn't the only one. I had never seen Chase so uncomfortable before. I decided to save him. "Of course Chase wants to kiss me. Just like he wants to kiss you." I smiled at his raised eyebrows. "I'm his sister too—didn't you know that?"

"You are?" Georgia's mouth dropped wide open. "Nuh-uh. You're teasing me, aren't ya?"

Chase leaned over and tousled her blonde curls. "Yep, Em's teasin' you. She's not your sister and she's wrong anyway. I'd never think of kissing her like that."

Sure. Just plunge the knife in deeper. It's a good thing I wasn't in love with the guy, or that would've really hurt.

For the rest of their visit, I managed to keep my grumpiness to myself. I focused on helping Georgia teach Clem some new tricks, which wasn't easy, but it kept the awkwardness of Chase at bay. I've never felt relief like I did when they finally left. Except it left the rest of my day wide open to think about Ethan Franklin.

So okay, I know I'm selfish sometimes, but his odd behavior really got to me. It wasn't that I was madly in love with him or something. Far from it. But he didn't have to treat me like I had the plague or something. What was the big deal about a stupid little kiss anyway? Did he go on some spiritual-cleansing Tibetan retreat and pledge to be a monk? *Like, what gives? Seriously.*

Finally, I figured out why his behavior bothered me so much. I was used to calling the shots. Yep, that was it. I was used to kicking boys to the curb—if you catch my drift. Like, why do you think I'd perfected my left hook, anyway? To keep rejects like Elton off me. *So that's what I don't get. Why isn't Ethan crawling all over me? Am I supposed to run after him to find out what it's like to be the pursuer? Like, is this some stupid reverse-psychology thing? Because if it is, he can take his monkish psychology major and shove it!*

"Emma? Your cell's ringing. Are you gonna answer it?"

"Huh?" I stared blankly up at my mom a moment and then over at my purse as it chirped at me. "Oh, thanks." I climbed off my bed and walked over to the purse to grab my phone. By the time I answered it, my mom had already left the doorway.

It was Hannah. "Hey, Emma, I was wondering what you're up to later tonight."

"Anything, if you're involved." Relieved, I smiled into my phone.

"Well, my mom and dad are heading down to Albuquerque for a getaway. I was wondering if you wanted company."

"Yes! That would be awesome. You should totally come and stay with us the whole weekend."

"Yay!" Hannah said. "I knew you would be all up for it."

"So did you survive last night? I mean, was the movie totally horrible?"

"Are you kidding? With Chase paying for everything? No way. He's an amazing date, seriously. I'm surprised you've never thought to go out with him."

"Me?" *Why is everyone suddenly wondering if Chase and I like each other?* "Not likely. I don't think I could stand being on a date with him."

I was irritated to hear Hannah laugh and then agree with me.

"So what time do you want me to come over?" she asked.

"Uh . . ." I flipped my hair out of my face. "Whenever, really. I'm totally going crazy at the moment, so if you're free, head over now."

"I can't. I'm finishing laundry. My mom would kill me if I left this load in the washing machine. But I'll be over ASAP."

"Okay. See ya then."

The phone went dead in my ear and I sighed for like the hundredth time that day. Falling back on my pillows, I wondered again what was wrong with me. Why was I more worried about Ethan being a dork, than me losing my heart over him? Wasn't he supposed to be my perfect match? Was I never, ever going to fall in love? The image of me as an old maid with dozens of cats flitted across my mind again, and I groaned and buried myself in pillows.

Much later, when Hannah made it over and went on and on about the wonderfulness of the movie date with Chase, it totally clicked. *Oh. My. Gosh. Why didn't I think of it before? It's perfect! Ethan Franklin and Hannah Smith! Eeeh. Okay, I'm gonna die happy now! It explains everything, like why I haven't been attracted to him, plus his awkwardness about kissing and stuff. He's totally shy, just like Hannah. Oh, and Hannah fallin' for older guys—he's older too. See? It's perfect. They were so meant to be together.*

There are moments in your life when everything clicks into place. You know, when all of the good karma flows your way and the planets, moon, and stars all align in perfect harmony to create one of those memorable moments of clarity. I was so having one of those moments. I sighed. *I'm a matchmaking genius, pure and simple! I knew all along I was destined to be something great. I mean, even my horoscope this month talked of my ability to move mountains and bend will to my way. Well, this is will bending my way.* I sighed again, and just when I was ready to throw myself back onto my bed and revel in my happiness . . .

"You haven't heard a word I've said, have you?" Hannah asked.

"What?" I caught myself from falling. "Of course I have. Chase was wonderfully sweet at the movie last night. Is there something else I've missed?"

"Ugh!" Hannah shook her head at me and buried her face in one of my pillows. "I knew it," came her muffled reply. "I knew you weren't listening to me for one minute!" She snapped her head back up and grinned slyly at me. "So what is it that has put that ridiculous smile on your face?"

Whatever. "I do not have ridiculous smiles." I smiled even more ridiculously at her.

She leaned forward. "Egad, Batman! You've thought of something, haven't you?" She snorted out a giggle.

I nodded my head and giggled back.

"Out with it!" Her eyes danced playfully and then she gasped. "I know what it is!"

"You do?" *This is getting better and better.*

"You think it's Chase who bought that camera for Cassidy, don't you?"

What? I blinked. "No!"

"Come on. Are you kidding me?" She sat back up. "Of course it's Chase. Who else would it be?"

I felt like I'd been slapped across the face. *As if Chase would EVER look at Cassidy. Taylor noticing her was bad enough, but Chase? No. Way.* I had to get that bizarre notion out of Hannah's mind immediately, so I said, "Puh-lease. Sometimes you scare me with the things you think about." I chuckled to sound more convincing. "Anyway, that wasn't what made me smile. What made me smile was the thought of linking your name with Ethan's."

Now it was Hannah who looked like she'd been slapped. "What in the world put that thought into your head? Have you totally lost your mind? Me and Ethan? Ethan and *me?* Yeah, right. If he likes anyone, it's you."

"Really?" I smiled, glad she was distracted. "I don't think so. I think he likes me—yes." I put my hand up to thwart off her attack. "But I know he doesn't *like* like me. We're just friends. And more than likely, that is all we'll ever be. I'm thinking his heart is open to new possibilities."

Hannah shook her head and stood up. "Let me get this straight. You think Ethan Franklin, the San Juan County four-wheeling champion, and I would be good together?"

"Yep!"

"Holy cow," Hannah grumbled as she lowered herself back down to my favorite overstuffed chair. "This is gonna be a long weekend."

I laughed. "Smile, Hannah. This is going to be an amazing weekend!"

TWENTY-ONE
♥

Hello. I'm a thief, and I'm here to steal your heart.

Okay, so more like an uneventful weekend. All we really did was play with my puppy and eat food. Then Hannah went home. See? Very uneventful, but still fun.

Once school started on Monday, I heard Ethan had already headed back to college. So much for matchmaking this time—we'd have to wait until Christmas.

Christmas! It's all anyone could think about. That word was everywhere. There were so many plans being made and so many parties and ideas, and everyone was getting in the spirit. My house was just as Christmas-tizzied as any—except more so, because Mom had started her frenzied planning for the ball. The invites had gone out before Thanksgiving. And now it was just down to the caterers, decorators, musicians, and Mom micromanaging the whole thing with an iron fist. Yep. The perfectionist Austenite had come out again.

School was, well, school. About halfway through December I realized I had a massive case of senioritis. Not good. The only good thing about senior year was Hannah. Thank goodness I had her as my BFF. Seriously, she kept me laughing and plowing through the subjects. Not to mention her wonderful study habits totally kept me from bombing classes. But there were definitely days when I wished America's school system was more like Great Britain's. It would be so cool to graduate at sixteen and start college right after that. Sometimes I felt so old, surrounded by all these younger, perky, happy teenagers still excited to be in high school. *Ugh. What I wouldn't give to be out of this place and in college already.*

"Hey you!" Hannah said as she tossed a chip in my direction. "What is up with you? You're daydreaming again."

"No. I wish." At least a daydream would be something productive. Anything was better than moping.

"Come on!" She tugged the sleeve of my coat from across the table. "I thought for sure you'd be all about getting a new dress for your mom's ball. Besides, my dad and mom have been totally cool about it and are letting me get my prom dress early so I can wear it there, too. So snap out of it already—we've got shopping to do!"

"Okay, you're right. I'm smiling." I smiled.

"Good. Now finish your lunch and let's go. This place is packed anyway, and we'll never be able to find anything if we don't hurry."

I looked around the food court and then down at my turkey-and-Swiss sub sandwich. Hannah had already finished hers and was now eating the last of her chips. *Yikes!* "Gimme a couple of secs, okay?"

"Fine. But hurry."

"Where should we go first?" I asked around a mouthful.

"Duh! Deb—where else?"

I nodded. *What was I thinking? Of course she'd wanna go there first.* Their clothes weren't high end, but they were uber cute and definitely affordable. It was one of the places Hannah had taken me on makeover day. She got a load of stuff from there.

"Hey, Em! What are you two doing here?"

Surprised to hear Chase's voice behind me, I nearly choked on a bite of my sub.

Hannah answered for me. "We're shopping for the ball. What are you guys doin'?"

Guys? I turned and saw Georgia grinning from her perch on Chase's shoulders. I took a couple more bites as she said, "We're going Chris-miss shopping! And Chase is gonna let me sit on Santa's lap and ev'rything. It's gonna be sooo cool."

"Wow." I swallowed and stood up so I could see her better. "And what do you want for Christmas?"

"That's easy. I want a kit-tar."

"A kit-tar?" I looked to Chase for translation.

"Guitar." He chuckled. "Who knew? We all figured she'd want a doll or something."

Hannah laughed. "Instead, Georgia's gonna be a rock star. That's awesome!" She stood and picked up her trash.

I downed the last bite of my sandwich. "Hey, Georgia, you want the rest of my chips?" I asked as I wiggled the bag in front of me.

"Yes! Yes! Yes! The cheesy kind is my favorite!"

"That's it." Chase swooped her off his shoulders in one smooth motion. "If you're gonna eat cheesy chips, you're not doing it near my head."

Hannah and I chuckled as I passed the bag over to the little girl. "Come on, Chase," I teased, "where's your sense of adventure?"

"Yeah, you never know—orange could be a good color on you," Hannah threw in.

He grinned. "True, true. Why didn't I think of that before?"

"Hurry, Chase!" Georgia tugged on his hand. "I'm starving! We have to eat first so we can see Santa, 'member?"

"Oh, yep. Santa. If you'll excuse me, I've got a demanding date."

"If we're on a date, then I want choc'late!" Georgia beamed up at him.

"See what I mean? Bye." Chase chuckled again as he was dragged off to stand in line for Chinese food.

"Cheesy chips and Chinese food? Hmm, that's a combo I think I'd rather pass on." Hannah made a face. "So are ya ready yet?"

"Yes, coming." I walked over and tossed my trash in the bin. "You're as bad as Georgia!"

"I'll be nice if you give me chocolate, too." Hannah smirked.

"Deal," I muttered.

Luckily, it only took three hours to make it out of the mall. I have to admit, two and a half of those hours were wasted by me. *Ugh.* I wasn't thrilled with my dress. It wasn't bad, just not as flattering as I'd hoped. I was almost tempted to wear one of the ones I already had, but—as always—the sparkle spoke to me. What girl doesn't love a new sparkly holiday gown? And this one was especially pretty. It was a flamboyant red and worked perfectly with Hannah's silver one. Really, when it came down to it, the two looked so cute together that I couldn't resist wearing it, just so Hannah and I could make a statement as we entered the ballroom together.

And statement we did! Two and a half weeks later as we walked under my mom's lit arch into the canopied ballroom of the Farmington Civic Center, we both burst into giggles at the reaction we caused. If the gasps of the crowd were anything to go by, Hannah and Emma had seriously broken some hearts. *Eeeh! Tonight is gonna be awesome!* Everyone who was anyone was there. And they all looked amazing.

Mom had one rule. If you weren't married, you had to come single. She wanted everyone to dance like they did back in Jane Austen's time, and to mix and mingle. So even though Chloe & Taylor and Carson & Madison were items, they weren't tonight.

"Hey, you two look so good!" squealed Chloe as she came up to us in her high heels and form-fitting dress.

"So do you! Check you out," I exclaimed.

"You look so posh, daw-ling, with your hair up like that!" Hannah laughed and sprang one of Chloe's loose curls. "I would give anything to have my hair do this."

"So when did you guys get back from Arizona?" I asked Chloe.

"Taylor and I drove up yesterday. School doesn't start for me until the middle of January, and Taylor's starts a few days after mine, so we're here again for the rest of the holidays."

"Cool!" Hannah and I cheered together.

"Yeah, I'm pretty excited. I just love being around my family during Christmas. My sisters are so much fun!" Chloe positively glowed.

I decided to keep my opinion of her family to myself. Instead, I shared a glance with Hannah and then asked, "So any news about Ethan? Is he coming tonight?"

"Ethan? Yeah." Chloe chuckled as Hannah rolled her eyes behind her. "He's been over at my house today, helping my dad decorate every square inch of the roof with Christmas lights. He's bringing Cassidy and Claire over later."

"Claire's coming too?" I tried to keep the surprise out of my voice.

"Yeah. Didn't you know? Your mom's so sweet she even invited Claire this year. She's wearing one of Cass's old dresses, but don't tell her I told you. She's been so excited all day—it's all I've heard about."

I'll bet.

"Excuse me, ladies, but I'm coming to steal Chloe away." Taylor's smooth voice startled us all. "They're getting ready to play our song."

"Hey!" I laughed as he took Chloe's hand. "Just remember you're single tonight. I want a dance, too."

"Yeah, yeah. You can be next," he agreed half-heartedly, his eyes still focused on Chloe.

Maybe he doesn't like Cassidy after all.

Hannah gasped. "Wow, the Anderson guys are totally hot."

"Aren't they?" I grinned at how flustered she looked. "There's something to say about that Anderson charm. Believe me, it's been tough living next door to them all these years."

"Yeah, so tough." She nudged me with her elbow. "I bet it was the hardest thing ever having to stare at those blue eyes every day."

"Whose blue eyes?"

Hannah and I spun around to see Chase smiling at us.

The punk. He heard every word we said. I was the first to recover. "We were talking about your little brother and sister, if you must know."

"Yep. Figures." Chase glanced down his tux to his designer shoes. "Georgia's got the looks and Taylor all the charm. Doesn't leave much for me, does it?" He impishly looked at me, nearly taking my breath away.

Wow! Chase Anderson is incredibly good looking. I felt like someone had just punched me in the gut—full force. I mean, my jaw dropped and everything. I don't know what he saw in my face, but whatever it was it made his gorgeous eyes glitter in response. Slowly, he raised his chin and walked toward me until he was standing about two feet away.

What is happening to me? Breathe. I gulped in a huge amount of air. Slowly, I pulled my face together enough to flash him a flirtatious grin. Just when I was about to make the biggest fool of myself, thankfully, Hannah saved me.

"Well, I don't know about Emma, but I'm thinking that tuxedo suits you."

"Really?" Chase asked, his eyes devouring mine.

"Yeah, you look good. Really," Hannah exclaimed.

Finally Chase wrenched his gaze away. "Thanks." He smiled vaguely at Hannah.

I took another huge breath and willed my hands to stop shaking. *For crying out loud, why am I acting like such an idiot? It's Chase, for Pete's sake. What is wrong with me?*

"So why aren't you dancing?" asked Hannah archly.

"Um . . ." Chase glanced briefly at me and then scanned the large crowd on the ballroom floor, before he sheepishly grinned at Hannah again. "Actually, I don't dance. I've never been good at it. Seriously. I didn't even go to prom. But hey, I can have Taylor ask you. He likes to dance."

"Oh." She looked disappointed, and I could tell Chase felt a little guilty.

"Emma?"

Carson was at my elbow. "Madison's dancing with my little brother. Are you dancing with anyone right now?"

"Me? N–no." I looked over at Hannah and saw her smile happily for me. "Are you okay, Hannah?" I really didn't want to leave her without a dance partner. And then it happened, like some horrible scene from a nightmare. Elton and his girlfriend Ashley walked right behind us in the middle of a group of people.

They were all laughing and talking about something, and none of us paid much attention until Ashley squealed loudly enough to be heard by us all.

"Oh, look! There's poor Chase again! Look how awkward he looks standing next to that Hannah chick." She broke away from her group and boldly walked right past me and up to him. "I'm single tonight, and I know you would much rather dance with someone who can hold her own." Ashley said the last part with a smirk in Hannah's direction.

The loser. Elton did tell her! I'm gonna kill him!

"You're right." Chase's voice sounded as cold as ice. "I would like to dance with someone who could hold her own. Especially around—" He choked on a word. I could tell it took every bit of self-control to contain his temper. "Hannah, I know you needed a few more minutes to talk to Em, but Carson's here to dance with her now. So are ya ready?"

"Ready?" I had never seen Hannah look so lost and frail before.

"To dance?"

"Oh yes! Let's get out of here." In an instant her stressed expression turned to grateful relief.

And my heart soared!

TWENTY-TWO

♥

Something tells me you're sweet.
Can I have a sample?

Watching Chase glide Hannah across the ballroom floor nearly caused my heart to burst. It's was true—he hated to dance, even more than I hated Elton. And that was saying something, since I really hated that jerk at the moment.

I could tell Chase and Hannah were causing quite a stir. I had just caught Mrs. Anderson's expression as Carson and I whirled past. To say she looked shocked to see Chase out on the dance floor was an understatement—she looked like she was going to cry.

Dang it! Don't get all teary-eyed or I will.

Another turn and I saw Hannah. She was absolutely beaming. In fact, I had never seen her so giddy. It was wonderful. *Chase is the most amazing, most awesome, nicest, sweetest, kindest, bestest person ever!* I couldn't repay him for his kindness if I tried every day for a hundred years.

"Well, I'm glad to see you're happy," Carson said. "I was afraid there for a sec that you were going to take that girl out."

"Really?" I giggled. Even Carson's reminder of Ashley's stupidity couldn't dampen my spirits. Everything was perfect in the world right in that moment.

"That was really nice of him," Carson said about the guy I was craning my neck to see.

Suddenly, I realized I wasn't being the ideal partner. "I'm sorry," I said ruefully, just before I looked up and saw Chase twirl Hannah out in front of him. *Aww. He's making this so perfect for her.*

Carson smirked at my expression. He must've given up trying to keep my attention, because after that he remained silent for the rest of the song. As soon as it ended, I quickly thanked him and then made a beeline straight for Chase. I couldn't wait to tell him how grateful I was.

Taylor intercepted me. "Hey, Emma, you ready for our dance?"

"Uh, would you do me a favor and dance with Hannah? I need to talk to Chase for a minute."

"Oh, okay. Sure. Where's she?"

"Over here. Chase, Hannah, wait up." They stopped in the middle of the dance floor. My Bradford smile beamed brighter than ever. I know, because I had never felt so good before. Taylor was right behind me; he spoke before I could make my tongue work.

"Hannah, would you mind dancing this next dance with me? I'll dance with Emma later."

"Oh, really? Wow! That'd be awesome!"

Her shock reminded me that she hadn't known these guys all her life like I had. She'd been awarded an opportunity that most girls in Farmington would've gladly given their right arms for—a chance to dance with both Anderson brothers. And actually, I can honestly say no one in history had been able to claim that feat, since Chase had never asked anyone to dance before. I shook my head, grinning like a complete idiot, as I watched her follow Taylor. They stopped about ten feet from us.

The next song began—it was another slow song. When I turned to look up at Chase, his expression left me a little breathless again. "Uh, I—I wanted to tell you thank you for—for what you did for Hannah."

"Oh, no worries. I survived." He shrugged and looked away as if it was no big deal, but I knew better.

"No, seriously." I clasped his hand in mine. "Thank you, Chase. I know how hard that was for you, so thank you."

His eyes seared into mine a moment before he dropped them and looked at our hands. I felt his palm twist ever so slowly and his fingers entwine with mine.

I let out a faint gasp as my heart stopped. Tiny tingles worked their way up to my elbow and then to the top of my shoulder.

"Em?"

"Yeah?" My voice cracked.

"We're in the middle of the dance floor."

I looked at the couples dancing all around us. "Oh."

"W–would . . ." He licked his lips and nervously glanced over at Taylor.

I could tell he'd rather be anywhere than where we were. "Come on." I tugged on his hand. "Let's get you off this floor." He didn't budge. "Chase?"

Our eyes locked. He gently pulled me toward him until I was standing just inches away. His eyes never left mine as I felt his other hand reach over and trail unhurriedly down my arm and cradle my fingers. His gaze glittered a moment—he seemed to be testing my reaction—before he brought my hand up and set it lightly on his shoulder.

My eyes widened, but I didn't say anything. I couldn't.

After he raised my other hand, which was entwined with his, he pulled me closer into him, and I realized his arm was wrapped around my waist.

I didn't think. I simply stepped into the strength and sanctuary of his chest. Before I knew what had happened, my head was resting quite comfortably on his shoulder. I felt him expel a large breath of air as I snuggled deeper into him.

And then we were moving. Carefully, preciously—as if I was made of spun glass—Chase's steps carried me away. I allowed my eyes to close. The sensation of his breathing and strength encompassed me as I floated on a cloud of moonbeams and wishes.

This was where I wanted to be, always, with my knight's protective arms guiding me wherever he wanted to go. In that moment, I knew I trusted Chase. I knew I needed Chase. I knew I—*Oh my gosh! Do I love Chase Anderson? Is that what has been stopping me from falling for anyone else? Is he the reason my heart wasn't free to love, because he had captured it years ago?* Just as quickly as the questions had come so had the answer. *He is! Holy cow.*

I stumbled. Instinctively, Chase pulled me closer and whispered, "I'm sorry," as if it was his fault.

There was so much I wanted to say to him. So many things I needed to think about first. But one thing was for certain, and it all made perfect sense. *I love Chase!*

"Em? Are you okay?" His baritone voice echoed through his chest and into my head.

He must've sensed a difference in me. "Yes." I smiled into his tuxedo jacket. "Everything's wonderful." *There couldn't be anything more perfect than this moment.*

Chase stopped. "Emma?" He pulled away from me a bit.

Reluctantly I raised my head. Thank goodness we were in a dark spot and not the center of the floor. I didn't want to leave his arms. Instead I tugged on the fingers he held. When he released them, I moved them up his shoulder to the back of his neck. My other hand was quick to join and my fingers locked in place behind him. Even in my heels, my forehead only came to his lips. But I wanted more than that. With a small push it was easy to maneuver his head down to mine.

"Em, wait—!"

But I didn't wait. I wanted to know what it felt like to kiss the guy I loved. My lips captured his.

Oh, it feels good! Millions of miniature fireworks exploded around my ears and behind my closed eyelids. It was all I could do to hold on and not collapse in a puddle at his feet.

It only took another second before Chase kissed me back. It was a good thing, too, because just as I was about to melt and slip away, I felt his arms wrap around my waist and brace me up.

I was lost. I wanted more.

And then it hit me. *This is Chase. Chase! As in, the way older guy who lives next door. The really, really successful guy who's been all over Europe. Who has a life —a life that probably doesn't revolve around me as much as I think. What in the world must he think about some silly high school senior kissing him in the middle of her mother's dance? Ack! What was I thinking? No wonder he wanted me to wait!*

Mortified, I pulled away.

He took a large gulp of air before lowering his brow to mine. His arms moved up from my waist to support my neck and head.

Here it comes. *He's gonna tell me all about how nice that was, but he isn't interested. And he'll only say it was nice because he doesn't want to hurt my feelings.* But he didn't say anything. He just breathed. He was breathing almost as hard as I was. Suddenly, he murmured, "Ethan's a fool!"

What? And then Chase's mouth devoured mine. Just like that. My heart soared. *He didn't tell me anything—he's kissing me! Eeeh! Chase Anderson is kissing me!*

TWENTY-THREE

♥

You look cold. Want me to hold you close?

"Ahem. Chase, your mother wants you."

We jerked apart to find Lionel Anderson staring right at us. My face flamed. *Oh my gosh! Oh my gosh! Oh my gosh!* I wished the floor would swallow me up.

"Are you sure, Dad?" Chase looked back down at me and then at his father to imply that now was not a good time to interrupt.

Just shoot me, I thought. *Seriously.*

"Son, as happy and as pleased as we are to see you out dancing on the floor, it would probably be a good thing if you didn't let your Sinatra feet go to your head. In other words, making out with Miss Bradford in a darkened corner of the ballroom could be a slap in the face to our very gracious hostess. Who, I might add, is your mother's best friend."

"Are you kidding me?" hissed Chase. "You've gotta bring this up now, in front of Emma?" He wrapped his arm protectively around me, but the damage was done. All I wanted to do was get away.

"Thanks for the dance, Chase, you're really good. Excuse me, Mr. Anderson." My Bradford smile beamed a little too brightly as I shrugged off Chase's arm and made my escape. I was across the room and almost out the wide double doors before I was aware of anyone.

"Emma! Wait up!"

It was Hannah. "Yeah?"

"Hey, did you see Taylor and me dancing? He's really good!"

"Really? Uh, no, I didn't see you guys."

"Oh, that's okay, I didn't see you either."

"Really? You couldn't see me and Chase? That's a relief!"

She looked at me funny for a moment, but we were both interrupted by Ethan.

"Hey, girls! I want you two to save me a dance, okay?"

"Sure!" Hannah was certainly in her element today.

"You game?" Ethan asked me.

"Yeah, sure. When?"

"Next slow song."

"Okay." *Whatever.*

"Hey, you don't look that great," Ethan observed. "Can I get you something?"

Air. I need air. Nice, cold Farmington winter air. "Nothing. I'm fine." I took a deep breath to steady my nerves and looked away. My eyes connected with my mom's. With one look, I knew she had witnessed that kiss. *Could this night get any worse? She's so never going to let me live it down. Making out with a guy at her ball in front of her friends—talk about nag fest.*

"Are you sure you don't need anything?" asked an obviously worried Hannah.

"I'm fine, really!" *I just want to be left alone.*

Right then Claire decided to join us. "What? Emma, are you all right? Cass and I were walking by and we heard—are you sure you're okay? I think Hannah is right. I think you need something. Don't you think she needs something, Ethan? You look awful, Emma. Just awful."

"Gee, thanks."

"Hey, why's the party over here?" Taylor asked.

I glanced up and saw Chloe, Madison, and Carson with him. Everyone was unconsciously blocking the stupid door. *For crying out loud. Can this get any worse?*

Of course Claire would be the first one to speak. "It's not a party. We're worried about Emma. She looks like she's sick or something—or maybe you've been dancing too much. Is that it? Have you been dancing too much? I did see you over in the corner with Chase—Oh! You two looked like you were . . . did his dad say something to you? My dad sure would've, especially if I was acting like that. I mean, is that even appropriate behavior? Who knows what—"

I lost it. "Just shut up, Claire! Seriously. We are all sick to death of hearing you talk anyway. I mean, is it possible for you to be quiet for ten minutes? Is it? Because as far as I can tell, you're always saying something. And it's usually something that shouldn't be said! So just keep your thoughts to yourself for once, and shut it! Okay?" With that, I pushed through the silent crowd and out the door. But I didn't get far. Of course not—this is my luck we're talking about here. In fact I had made it just to the outer door of the lobby when I heard Chase's voice behind me.

"Emma!"

I pushed the door open and spun around. He was jogging toward me. From the look on his face, it was clear he wasn't happy. With a maneuver just short of a shove, he propelled me through the door into the frigid night air. And then he whirled on me.

"What was that about?" he bellowed.

"What?"

"That—that outburst to Claire!"

He was there? I had never seen Chase look so upset before. "Oh, come on!" I snorted. "As if you haven't wished a hundred times to say the exact same thing to her. Don't give me that look! She's annoying, and she needed to be told. Honestly, I've done you a favor. You can thank me later. I'm outta here." I turned to flounce away, but he grabbed my elbow and jerked me back.

"Yes, you're out of here. I don't know what has come over you, but believe me, whatever I felt earlier is gone. You are just like what I always thought you were—a spoiled, selfish brat who couldn't care less about anyone other than herself."

"What? As if! You know what?"

"What do I know, Emma? Huh? What do I really know of you? Just that you're more worried about what people are saying about you and what they're thinking about you—so much so that you don't even know yourself!"

Of all the—"Just drop it, Chase. I've heard enough!" I tried to yank my arm away, but he held fast.

"Do you have any idea why I'm mad? Why I would dare to contradict the great Emmalee Bradford?"

I glared at him and tried to break free again.

"No?" He dragged me toward him until we were just inches apart, until I could feel the warmth of his body. "You know, had she been Elton's girlfriend, or any of your cheerleader friends, or someone who was your age, fine—throw a fit. It would make you look stupid, but hey, if you want to be stupid that's your prerogative. But when it involves younger girls like Claire, then yeah, you're gonna see me get involved."

He closed his eyes and heaved a sigh. "Emma, Claire Hart is fifteen years old. She worships you. She thinks you're the most amazing girl on the planet. Everyone knows it, too. *Everyone.* It's all she talks about. Just ask them. 'Emma is so pretty. Emma is so cool. Emma is so nice.' Yes, Emma, she loves you. *You!* And what do you do? The first time she is finally invited to come to your mother's ball—the first time she's allowed to dress up and feel as pretty as you—you humiliate her in front of everyone. You've completely shattered and ruined that girl in one stupid, weak moment. I have never known you to behave so badly before! And the worst thing is, you won't even remember what you've said in ten minutes from now."

Chase raked his free hand through his hair. "Look, I'm sorry, okay?" He loosened his grip from my arm, but his eyes continued to pierce mine. "I—I know this is probably going to make you hate me forever. And if that's the case, fine. It needed to be said. I just— I can't believe you treated Claire like that."

His anger I could take. How many times had I matched him in verbal battles? How many times had I held my own? But his disappointment, his hurt—I couldn't take that. Breathless, I watched his eyes accuse me of every horrible deed I had ever done. He was right. I was selfish and cruel and no better than Ashley Templeton.

With a weary sigh, he lowered his eyes to the frost-covered pavement. "Em, I can see now that I just want you to be someone you're not." His pain-filled gaze met mine briefly. "I wish you were someone I could really love. I needed that—needed her— but that girl isn't here. I'm sorry." With that, he turned and made his way back up to the lobby door.

My breath came out in little white puffs as my heart fell to my feet. I watched Chase kick a pebble off the mat and then enter into the building. The door swung closed behind him, and he never looked back.

I scooped up the bottom of my long gown and ran to my car. Thankfully, I made it before the first tear fell. It was all I could do to get the door open and lunge into the driver's seat. In the cold confines of the car, I realized my purse was still inside the building. There was no way to turn on the engine and get warm. I was going to freeze to death in my own car!

That did it. The dam broke. Miserable tears sprung to my eyes and trailed down my cheeks. I had never felt more alone. And the only one I had to blame was myself. My own stupid, horrible self.

Chase hates me. The only guy I have ever loved hates me! How could life be so cruel? How could I have been so cruel?

I don't know how long I sat in the car before I heard a knock on the glass next to me. The windows were embarrassingly steamed up and my head hurt from crying until I couldn't cry anymore.

Someone knocked again, louder this time. Reluctantly, I pulled myself out of my frozen cocoon and opened the door. Chase was there with my purse. One look at his face and I could tell he felt as wretched as I did.

"Em, why didn't you tell me your purse was in there? Have you been out here in the cold all this time?"

I blinked, grateful I was able to do that much.

With a muttered curse, he pulled me out of the car. His warm fingers tingled on my bare arms. "You're freezing," he exclaimed.

As if I didn't already know that.

"How could you be so stup— stubborn?"

I tried to smile when I realized he had just stopped himself from calling me stupid again.

He mumbled something else under his breath and removed his tuxedo jacket. The warmth of the smooth satin lining as it slid over my stiff arms was indescribably delicious. After he got me in the jacket, he pulled my shoulders toward him and wrapped his arms around me, obviously trying to give me as much body heat as possible. It was the most amazing sensation I had ever felt.

I don't know if it was the shock of the sudden warmth to my system, or the cold air on my ears and cheeks, but I began to shiver. Big, teeth-chattering shivers. Had I been more aware of myself, I would've probably died of embarrassment, but the only thing I could think of was getting warm.

"Dang!" Chase quickly swooped me up in his arms and slammed my car door shut. With quick strides he made it to his truck in seconds. Before I knew what was happening, I was in the passenger side of the cab—still in his arms. I was jolted slightly as he double-checked the emergency brake, threw the truck out of gear, and started it up. Soon, the cold air that blasted through the vents grew warm and comforting. After a few minutes, my shivering slowed and I began to thaw.

"What is it about you?" Chase murmured in my hair after a long silent moment.

"Hmm?" I asked lazily.

"I can't figure out how anyone can be so independent, yet so needy at the same time."

Another shudder escaped and I snuggled closer. "What would I do without you?" I asked, relishing in the strong heartbeat I felt beneath his white shirt.

"I don't know." He chuckled softly to himself before he inhaled sharply. "I'm almost afraid of leaving again. I'm not sure you'll be here when I get back."

Yeah, most likely I'll have killed myself somehow without my knight to rescue me. "What do you care, anyway?" My fingers fiddled with the creased folds in his shirt.

"I'm going to Phoenix for a while, right after Christmas."

My fingers stilled. "What?"

"I've thought about it long and hard the past hour and—and I need to get away. There's just too much . . . too much tension here."

No. I blew it. He's leaving because of me. My eyes began to prick with tears. "Chase?" I said while I could still speak. "Don't go."

I felt him inhale against the top of my head again—a deep, ragged breath. "I have to."

One tear fell and I shook my head into his chest. "No, you don't. You don't. You promised six months. You promised. And it's only been three."

"I'll come back before I head back out to Spain next year to say goodbye, okay?"

The tears fell. I couldn't help it. I was such a wreck. If I could take back anything—anything—it would be this day. *Why did I have to realize today of all days—the day I ended up ruining everything—that I loved him? I would've much rather had him here with me every day, not knowing that I loved him, than gone away because I did, and knowing he hated himself for it. Obviously, he regretted getting as close to me as he did. Why shouldn't he hate himself? I'm an immature little baby. I don't deserve anyone like him in my life. He's better than anything I could ever amount to.*

All at once I wanted Chase gone—a thousand miles away—but still here holding me at the same time.

His hands started to trail lightly over my back as he gently rocked back and forth. I knew he felt my wet tears on his shirt and was trying to make me feel better. And I tried to be brave, but it didn't work. Fresh, muffled sobs wracked my body.

"Shh," he said softly. "Come on, Em, don't do this. It's hard enough for me to leave as it is."

Then don't go! I wanted to scream it at him, but I couldn't bear to hear his rejection again.

After my sobs died down, I felt his lips rub across my hair. "Em?" He pulled back a little and kissed my forehead.

Hmm... I like that.

"Emma?" Tenderly he eased my shoulders away from him and kissed my nose. I held my face up for more and he obliged, kissing one cheek and then the other. "You are so beautiful."

I grinned up at him and opened my eyes. "Liar." With my tear-stained face, I couldn't have been uglier if I tried.

His eyes searched mine. At first I thought he was going to change his mind about leaving—about me—but then I realized he was only checking to see if I was okay. He wouldn't leave me like this if he could help it.

I fought back another onslaught of tears as I memorized his handsome face. *I love him. I love him so much!*

Pulling myself together, I sat up straight and forced my mouth to smile. "I hope you have a wonderful time in Phoenix. You'll be missed." *More than you know.*

Chase scanned my features. "Thanks." He knew exactly what I was doing.

Our conversation was over. What more could either of us say? He needed to leave and I needed him to stay, and neither of us could really compromise. We were doomed. I quickly blotted out the image of me with knitting needles and cats, and shrugged my way out of his jacket.

"Do you want me to take you home?" he asked as I handed it to him.

"No." I gave him a quick smile and then looked down at my hands.

"Do you know how to drive a stick?"

What? "Yeah."

"Here." He set me down in front of the steering wheel. "Drive this. It's already warm. You can park it at your house and I'll pick it up in the morning. I'll drive yours. Did you bring Hannah with you?"

Hannah? "Hannah!" *I forgot all about her!* "Yes, I did."

"Don't worry." Chase stilled my hands from reaching for the door. "It's no big deal. I'll take her home in your car."

Why does he have to be so great? "Okay, thanks." I looked down at the hands he was holding and back up at him.

It was time to go, but he stayed where he was. My heart pounded in my throat when I caught the familiar sparkle in his eyes. Slowly, he raised one hand and brushed an errant curl off my face.

That was all it took. I don't know who moved first—all I know was I was wrapped up in his arms and he was kissing me again. Really kissing me. It was wonderful! It was horrible! Our last farewell, our bon-voyage kiss. It was the worst, most miserable thing to do to a girl, yet the most delicious and precious moment in all of history.

Chase broke away first. He gasped for air, then shook his head and stared at me. "How could anything so wrong for me, feel that good?" he muttered. Just before he opened the door and got out of the truck, he looked up at the roof and said, "I'm being punished, aren't I?"

No. I am.

TWENTY-FOUR

♥

So, what do I have to do to get a hug out of you?

I was in trouble and knew it the second I woke up. *Mom is gonna kill me.* The old me would've rolled onto my other side and put it off as long as possible, pretending I was still asleep. But this was the new me, and it was time to face what I'd done. With a sigh, I rolled out of bed.

In record time, I was out of the shower and dressed. I didn't bother with makeup. That was hard, but I didn't want to hide behind anything anymore. It wasn't worth it. I was who I was, and Chase was right. It was time I faced myself. All of me. The real me. Emmalee Glumm. No more hiding behind a fancy last name, my stepdad's money, or my killer smile. *If I'm lucky, by the time this day is over, I may still have a few friends left—but then again, maybe not.* One thing was for certain—whoever chose to stay by me would never be taken for granted again.

I could hear my mom in the kitchen as I went down the stairs. After taking some deep breaths, I walked through the doorway. "Hey, Mom."

She looked up, scanning my very normal-looking clothes and face before dumping a bunch of fruit into the blender. She didn't say a word as she turned it on. The sound of the loud motor filled the room. I sat on a bar stool, not sure what to do. After a couple of more seconds, Mom turned off the blender and poured herself a tall glass of smoothie. When she turned and saw me still in the kitchen, she poured me one as well and brought it over.

Her peace offering before reading me the riot act made me feel even worse. "Thanks," I mumbled as I took a sip.

She watched me as she took a long drink from her glass. When she set it back on the counter, she finally spoke. "Well, dear, what do you have to say for yourself?"

Nothing. Everything. "I'm sorry, Mom. I'm really sorry."

"Are you?" She didn't look convinced.

All at once I felt unbelievably small. I nodded my head and looked down at my smoothie.

"Dang it, Emmalee!" Mom was used to me arguing with her, and I could tell she was ready for a fight. "Do you have any idea of the mess you left me with last night? How humiliating that was for me and *our* guests? Could you have behaved any worse?" She paused. "Honestly, I want to know!" Now she was yelling. "Could you have?"

My stepdad ran up from the basement, no doubt wondering what was wrong. One look at me and he quickly stepped forward and wrapped his arm around his wife's waist to show his support.

Yep. That's me, the monster who's so evil people have to come in pairs to attack. My finger rubbed the top of the glass and I shook my head. "I'm sorry, Mom and Dad." I looked up at both of them. "I know I was awful last night—I know it. It's haunted me for hours now."

"Honey, this isn't something you can blow off," said my stepdad. "People were genuinely offended. It was really bad." He looked down at my mom and patted her shoulder. "Actually, it was so bad we're thinking of canceling the balls altogether."

"What? No! You can't do that. Mom loves them."

She sighed. "Emmalee, I don't think anyone will come next year, even if I did throw one."

Was it really that bad?

Looking weary, Mom rubbed her face. "You know, when you tell the future in-laws of the Andersons to shut up, that's basically social suicide. Emma, it's over. You are going to have to grow up. I didn't think it could get much worse when you practically forced Chase to kiss you in the middle of that dance—"

I winced.

"—but I was wrong. I have never seen tears like those of poor Claire Hart. Never. The few people who didn't hear your unfortunate outburst quickly heard an exaggerated version in no time. Thank goodness only a select few, from what we can tell" —she glanced up at my stepdad for conformation— "actually witnessed your, uh, kisses with Chase."

My stepdad cleared his throat, and I knew what was coming next wouldn't be pretty. "We've talked it over, Emma, and your mother and I have come to the conclusion that you should be treated the same way you treated Claire last night."

What in the—? "What does that mean?"

My mom jumped in. "It means, dear, that if you think Claire is too young and immature to have access to certain places and information, then so are you."

This doesn't sound good. "Okay?"

"As of today, you are losing your privileges. You will have no phone, no internet except for schoolwork, no car, no dates, no parties or sleepovers—"

"What? Are you kidding me?" I nearly spilled my smoothie. "Come on, isn't that a bit overdramatic? I never told Claire she couldn't do all those things—I only told her to keep her mouth shut."

"She's arguing," my stepdad remarked. "You said she would argue, but I didn't believe you." He patted my mom on the shoulder. "Okay then, I won't stop you—you can take her final privilege away."

Uh-oh. When I saw the look on her face, I knew it was bad. "Mom, what is he talking about?"

She sighed and wrapped her arms around herself. "Emma, we did think of one more thing, in case you didn't see the seriousness of the situation. One more privilege we have granted you, that we feel you may not be mature enough to handle right now. I was so angry last night I was going to take it away from you right then—along with the rest—but Adrian convinced me to wait and see how you reacted first, to see if you were remorseful enough."

"I am remorseful! I promise you, I am!" I protested, trying to remain calm. "I've changed so much from last night you wouldn't even recognize me."

My mom shook her head sadly. Whatever people had said the night before must've been just awful, because she had a steely look in her eyes that I'd never seen in all my eighteen years. But honestly, I'd never thought she'd be that cruel, until she actually said it.

"Bring Clementine down. She's going back to the Andersons today."

What?

"Emma, you've lost the privilege of owning a puppy."

"NO!"

"Yes."

"Mom, no. Please, you can't. Please, Mom!" *It's all I have of Chase.*

"Emmalee Elaine, go now. If you bring the dog down immediately, I will let you take her over to their house yourself. But if she isn't down here in five minutes, I'll do it for you."

I ran. What else was I supposed to do? I was the new Emmalee. The Emmalee Glumm that didn't get special privileges or rights. The realization of what I had done hit me then, really hit me. In one stupid, weak moment I had lost everything—literally everything I'd ever loved or cherished—other than my family.

Once I got to my room and saw little Clem sleeping in her bed, I burst into tears. The last thing I wanted to do was take her over to the Andersons myself, but I would always regret it if I didn't say a proper goodbye. Carefully, I collected as many of her things as I could find and placed them next to her in her bed. I threw on my jacket and hefted the doggy bed. I carried it down the stairs and out the back door, which my mom held open for me.

Slowly, I made my way through our backyard, through the Andersons' backyard, and then up their porch to the back door. The knock sounded as hollow as my heart. Too quickly, Mrs. Anderson opened the door.

"Come in, Emma. Your mom called to say you were coming." She gave me a knowing look.

I tried to smile. *Dang. There are days I really wish she wasn't my mom's best friend.*

"Well, Georgia's going to be real happy." I could tell Mrs. Anderson was trying to lighten the mood.

"I'm glad. I'm sure going to miss this little dog." At the sound of my voice, Clementine woke up and bounded into my chest. *Ahh!*

"Here, let me take the bed from you," Mrs. Anderson said. "You keep the puppy and I'll follow you up to Georgia's room."

"Thanks." I chuckled when Clem eagerly kissed me. I couldn't see Chase anywhere but was afraid to ask if he was around. *No use bringing up any more reminders of last night. Unless—?* As I started up one side of the double cascading staircase, I decided to put my new Emmalee Glumm to the test.

"I'm really sorry about last night, Mrs. Anderson." I kept walking, not looking back to see her reaction. I wasn't that brave. Instead, I quickly filled in before she could say anything. "I don't know what you saw or heard, but I am terribly sorry if you were offended by any of my actions. And I hope you never blame my parents for my, uh, stupidity."

"That was very well said, Emma." Chase's mom sounded surprised. "I hope this will all pass over quickly, for your sake."

"Thanks," I mumbled, unsure what else to say.

Georgia was in her room when we got there. "Emma! Emma!" She squealed as she ran over to me. "You did bring her!"

Her enthusiasm made me feel a little better. I mean, if I couldn't keep Clementine, she might as well go back to someone who loves her.

"Can I hold her? Please, please, please?"

"Sure." I smiled and bent down. The puppy went happily into Georgia's arms, wagging her little tail. "Now, you're going to take real good care of her, right, Georgia?" I grinned and scratched Clementine's ears.

"Yep! We're gonna be best friends."

"Can I come and see her sometime?" *Er, when I'm not under house arrest?*

"Yeah. We can even have puppy tea parties."

I blinked back a couple of tears. "That sounds awesome. I can't wait."

After a quick goodbye to Mrs. Anderson and Georgia, and an almost tearful goodbye to Clementine, I left.

My day was just beginning. When I got home, I quickly baked a batch of my mom's famous cookies, grabbed my coat and hat, and walked the three miles to the Hart house. I probably could've gotten my mom to take me—or at the very least, relent and let me drive over there—but the new Emmalee Glumm needed to walk. *If Cassidy can do it, so can I.* Besides, I really wanted to get my thoughts in order before I apologized to Claire and her family.

At the Harts', I took another deep breath and rang the doorbell, holding the cookies in front of me on a pretty plate wrapped in cellophane.

Chloe answered, her friendly smile dying on her face as she realized it was me.

Oh dear. This is going to be even harder than I thought. Hesitantly, I smiled back and asked, "Is Claire here? I came to apologize."

Chloe folded her arms and stared at me, probably trying to determine if I was being sincere. Finally, she nodded her head and said, "I don't know if she wants to see you, but I'll ask, okay?"

"Okay." *It's better than nothing.*

"Wait here."

I waited. After a couple of minutes, the door swung open and Claire burst out of it. In a complete surprise, she put her arms round me.

"Emma! I'm so sorry," she exclaimed. "I'm so, so sorry! Please say you'll forgive me! Please say you don't hate me anymore! I promise I'll never, ever talk again!"

I am *a monster! I'm a terrible, horrible monster!* Tears sprang to my eyes again as I wrapped my arms around her, dropping the plate of cookies on the porch. Claire was still apologizing, but I couldn't hear much of it over the pounding of my heart. Finally, I composed myself enough to say what I needed to.

"No, Claire. Stop, sweetie. Stop," I said as I gently dislodged myself from her grasp. "You can't apologize anymore. I won't let you."

She pulled back farther. "I—I can't?"

"No." I smiled at her expression and wiped the tears from my cheeks. "I'm here to beg your forgiveness—not the other way around."

"You . . . you are?" She looked so stunned a new wave of guilt washed over me.

"Yes, Claire." I held onto her shoulders and looked right at her. "I'm your friend. I love you. You are a wonderful, amazing person. And I was dreadfully wrong last night. I was evil and mean and spiteful and every other horrible word you can imagine. I don't know why I said what I said, but believe me, I have felt miserable ever since. I mean, completely horrid. I came here today expecting you to never want to speak to me, but I never expected you to feel like this. Claire, please believe me when I say you did nothing wrong. It was all my fault.

"If I could take back one moment in time, it would be last night when I said those terrible things to you. I don't deserve your apology. I don't even deserve your acceptance of mine, but I had to come here today anyway. And just for the record, you're not bad, Claire. Your energy and excitement are completely contagious. Do me a favor and don't ever change, okay? Life wouldn't be the same without your eagerness and happiness."

For once she just nodded her head. She didn't say anything. She didn't have to—her miraculous smile said it all. I was forgiven. And right then, there was nothing more valuable to me in all the world than the love and forgiveness of Claire Hart.

TWENTY-FIVE

♥

You are the reason men fall in love.

The rest of the Hart family wasn't as forgiving as Claire, but I could tell my visit went a long way toward smoothing things over. I repeatedly apologized until I was sure they were sick of hearing me, but I wanted to let them know how genuine I was. I had changed. I was different. I wanted them to see that I would never make the same mistake again.

On my way home, I decided to take a quick detour to Hannah's house and apologize to her as well. If I needed any friend right now, it was her. Plus, in case she'd been trying to text me or email me, I wanted to let her know I wasn't ignoring her.

By the time I got to her house, it was almost two o'clock.

"Hey, Emma, I was just getting ready to come see you," she said, opening the door for me.

I smiled as I walked in. "You were?"

"Yeah. You wouldn't believe what just happened to me—I mean, like just now!" Hannah looked completely freaked out.

All at once everything else flew from my mind. "What happened? Are you okay?"

"I'm wonderful!" She twirled in front of me and wrapped her arms around her waist.

"Hannah?" I'd never seen her so happy before.

"You won't believe it. I mean, you'll probably be mad at me, but I don't care. I don't care what anyone says. Because I just got off the phone with Martin Roberts—and we're going out!"

"Really?"

"Yep. And there is no way you're going to ruin this moment for me, so don't even try."

"I . . . no! This is great news. I'm so happy for you. Really." *And baffled, too.* "How—how did it happen?"

"Chase." Hannah smiled and began to giggle as she waltzed into the living room.

"Chase?" I followed.

"Yeah. He told Martin that if he really loved me, he shouldn't let me go without a fight."

"You're kidding."

"Nope. So Martin called this morning to fight for me." With a dreamy look in her eyes, she sat down on the couch. "I decided to let him win this time."

{♥}

Once I got back to my house, I heard a deep voice coming from the kitchen

"Hey, Emmalee." My mom was all smiles as I walked in. "Look who came to see you."

"Hi, Chase." I took off my coat and tossed it on the small breakfast table. "I thought you'd be home packing." *Great, Emmalee, just bring it up.*

"I am, later."

"I'll leave you two alone." My mother smiled up at him like he was the long-lost prodigal son. *Apparently he's been forgiven for kissing me—or maybe she doesn't blame him at all. Figures.*

I waited until she left before I casually asked, "So, did you need something?"

Chase got right to the point. "When did you find out you had to give up Clem?"

"Today."

He shook his head and ran his fingers through his hair. "Are you okay? How do you feel?"

Like someone has just taken a knife and stabbed me in the heart about thirty times. You? "Fine."

"Em-ma."

"Emmalee, actually."

"What?"

I walked over to the cupboard and pulled down a glass so I wouldn't have to look at him. "I've decided to go by Emmalee from here on out."

"But why? I like Emma."

I leaned over the sink and ran the cold water. "Because I'm not Emma anymore. She's gone." Once my glass was full I turned toward him, but I still didn't look up. Instead, I studied the pretty way the sun shone through the tumbler from the window above the sink.

"I don't understand," Chase said. "What happened?"

"It was simple. I thought about what you'd said last night and you were right." I glanced down at my shoes. "I, uh, thought it was time to grow up. So I'm doing it. Well, I'm gonna try, at least." Shaking my head, I tried to will the memories away. "I was horrible last night. Completely the worst version of myself

I've ever had to face. I didn't like what I saw. I'm surprised you stuck around long enough to help me see what an ogre I've become."

"Emma." Chase took a step toward me. "I never meant— I don't know how you've even dealt with me. I have been awful—horrible—to you. Has there been a day when I haven't chewed you out for something?"

I smirked. "I'm sure there has been, but I can't think of one."

"Look, the reason I was so mad was because I thought you were actually turning into Ethan. I thought you'd picked up his habit of just saying whatever he wants, no matter who's around."

"Oh no. Last night was all me, unfortunately. I can't blame Ethan for anything."

"Yes, you can."

I took a sip of my water. "No, I can't, Chase. Look, do you want some hot chocolate or something?"

He walked over to a stool and sat down. "Sure, I never turn down chocolate. But actually, I have news about Ethan, and it's not the best news. And I—uh, don't know how to say it."

My hands froze in midair as I lifted the kettle. "What news?" *Could this day get any worse?*

"Well, Taylor was talking to Chloe, and Chloe had been talking to Cassidy, and Cassidy said—"

"Okay, out with it already." I marched to the faucet and began to fill the kettle.

Chase took a deep breath and blurted, "Ethan and Cassidy are secretly going out."

The kettle dropped with a bang into the sink. "What?" I quickly picked it up.

"They've been going out for almost two years now."

I whirled around. "Two years? Ethan and Cassidy? Are you messing with me?"

"No." Looking miserable, Chase glanced down at his hands. "They've been secretly going with each other since Ethan's senior year when he took Cassidy to prom. Apparently, she's been grounded from dating anyone because my reject cousin Blake tried to get with her. So they've been going behind her parents' backs. Ethan and Cassidy have an email, text, and cell-phone relationship. It's been pretty hard on both of them, especially when he has to pretend to like other people so no one figures it out."

I gasped. "No wonder the dork couldn't kiss me!" I smiled. "He so could've said something, you know. I would've totally helped them."

"As far as I know, Chloe just found out herself. I guess Cassidy is really good at— Wait, you're laughing?" Chase looked completely shocked. Like seeing me laugh in the kitchen was a totally foreign thing to him.

It made me laugh even harder. It felt wonderful to laugh. *To think all this time I have been basing my spinsterhood on a guy who was already taken. That is so my luck.*

"So—so you're not mad?" Chase asked.

The look on his face was so cute I had to giggle. "Why would I be mad?" *He's such a weirdo. Of all the things to be mad about, Ethan and Cassidy are way off my list.*

"So you don't have a thing for him?"

I snorted. "For Ethan? What, are you high? As if I would have a thing for Ethan Franklin!" I shook my head and pulled the overflowing kettle from the sink and turned off the tap. After pouring a bit off the top, I carefully carried it over to the stove and set the lid on, then put the burner on high. I turned around to find Chase standing right in front of me.

"Oh—!"

It was all I could get out before his lips caught mine. *Holy cow!* Automatically, my hands clutched his elbows and then slowly wound their way up his shoulders and around his neck.

He broke away. "Em?"

"Yeah?"

"Ask me to stay. You shouldn't" —he closed his eyes briefly— "but ask me to stay anyway, and I will."

"Stay. Please stay."

When he opened his eyes, they were the bluest I had ever seen them. "Really? Just like that. You don't hate me? You don't wish I was in Arizona, or back in Spain or somewhere?"

Are you for real? "No."

"Why?"

"Why do you want to stay?" I asked.

"Let's go for a walk."

"Now?" *I just got back from a walk.* But already I was turning off the stove.

"Yeah, just out back. Come on." Chase went to the table and collected my jacket. He held it out for me as I slid my hands through the arms. After I zipped the coat, he offered his hand to me. I stared at it.

I couldn't believe he was there, holding his hand out for me. It was like I had died and gone to heaven. I knew then that if I put my hand in his, my life would never be the same. Everything I had ever thought, or planned, or dreamed up until that moment was going to change forever. *I can't wait!* With a giddy grin on my face, I stepped forward and slipped my small, manicured hand into his larger, smooth one. My eyes met his. *Sheesh. How could I have been so blind to how incredible he is?*

He matched my grin and tugged me closer. We wandered down to Mom's gazebo. It was wonderful, for once, to just talk about anything and everything—or nothing at all—and be content in each other's company.

Once we sneaked through the back gate between our properties, I asked, "Where are you taking me?"

Chase squeezed my hand. "You'll see. There's something I want to show you."

"Hmm . . . mysterious." I chuckled softly and rested my head on his shoulder as we leisurely followed the path that led to the pond. And then he stopped, right next to the dock. "There," he said.

"You wanted to show me the pond?" I grinned up at him. "Hate to break it to you, but I've seen this place before."

Smiling, he leaned down and placed his forehead on mine. "Not through my eyes you haven't."

"Prove it."

I wasn't sure what he was going to do, but I didn't expect him to turn me around so that my back was facing him and then wrap his arms around me. "See where that large oak tree is back there?"

He didn't have to point. I knew the tree well. "Yeah."

"Now look about twenty feet from the foot of that tree, straight into the pond."

"Okay."

"What do you see?"

"Cold water." I chuckled.

"Is that all?"

And then it hit me. *Why did Chase bring me here?* I shuddered and took a step back into him. Horrid images from my nightmares flew into my mind. "It's where—it's where—"

"It's where I fell in love with you."

What? The nightmares fled. "Y–you did?"

He wrapped his arms tighter around me. "Of course I didn't know it then. All I knew was I couldn't live if anything were to happen to you. My heart stopped beating that day. Just seconds more and you would've been gone. Do you know when it began to beat again?"

I bit my lip and shook my head no.

"When you kissed me on that dance floor."

"Really?"

"Well, when I got back from Spain, I felt a faint beat, but I tamped it down and hid it away. It wasn't until you kissed me and nearly knocked me over that it began to beat—really beat—and loudly. I've always been drawn to you. Always. I just didn't realize why until you kissed me. I needed you—you were who I was looking for."

He's so amazing! "But why did you want to go back to Phoenix? Wait! Don't answer that." I closed my eyes as misery washed over me again.

"Emma?"

"Emmalee."

"Emma-lee, what do you see when you see that spot in the pond now?"

Slowly I opened my eyes. The sunshine sparkled on the clear water. "The most beautiful water in the whole world."

"I love you, Emmalee Glumm," Chase whispered in my ear. "Do you think you could put up with me for a while?"

Slowly, I turned around within the circle of his arms and laid my ear against his chest. His strong, steady heartbeat made me unbelievably happy. "I love you, Chase, and I'll put up with you forever if you promise to always be my knight in shining armor."

"Done," he murmured in my hair.

I grinned and snuggled closer. "It's a real good thing you're hot, isn't it?"

He chuckled and pulled back, his eyes searing into mine. "That's my Emma, always a brat."

"It's Emmalee." I giggled. "And I prefer the term 'princess.'"

Chase threw his head back and laughed. "You would!" Then he swooped me up in his arms and tossed me over his shoulder.

"Don't you dare throw me into that pond!" I shrieked. "I swear, Chase, I'll kill you!"

"Knowing you, I wouldn't doubt it." He headed up the path.

"Where are we going?"

"Well, Your Majesty, I thought the first order of the day would be to rescue your dog."

"Clementine! Really? But how?" I twisted to see his face but it didn't work. "Chase, put me down!"

He ignored me. "Your mom seemed to think you'd learned your lesson when you went over to the Harts, and she wanted to make sure I took you back to get your puppy."

"But what about Georgia?"

"She figured she wouldn't get to keep the puppy forever. As soon as I saw her with Clem, I told her we were going to take her back anyway."

"Really?"

"Yep. What did you think your mom and I were talking about earlier?"

"I have no idea. Ugh. Put me down, Chase. I'm gonna get sick."

"Almost there."

"Are you going to be like this forever? I'm not sure I can handle it. As far as I'm aware, princesses don't get lugged around by their knights anyway."

"Haven't you ever seen *Shrek?*"

"*Shrek?*" I laughed. *Great!* "That is where you're getting your inspiration from—the movie *Shrek?*"

"Hey, you're the one who brought up my looks, not me."

Good grief! "Your handsome looks—not ogre looks."

Chase laughed as he gently set me down on the porch. For a moment he just stared at me. "Beauty is in the eye of the beholder." His gaze burned into mine.

I gave him my new Emmalee Glumm smile and captured his hand that cupped my cheek. "Just as long as you remember that, we'll be good."

He leaned in and whispered against my lips, "Emmalee, you're beautiful. Can I hold you?"

I sighed and melted into his arms. What else was I supposed to do? It's not every day a girl hears Chase utter a pickup line.

It just goes to show that even though everything may seem perfect, it takes a whole lot of work to get it there. I was so busy trying to change everyone else that I had no idea I was the one who needed the most help. Thankfully, I was able to realize that in time to open my eyes and my heart to allow my knight his greatest rescue of all.

ABOUT THE AUTHOR

Jenni James is the mom of seven rambunctious children. They've lived in Portugal, England, and Utah, and now make Farmington, New Mexico, their home. When Jenni isn't writing, she's chasing her kids around the house and exploring the world to find new romantic stories to create. She is the author of the Jane Austen Diaries as well as the Jenni James Faerie Tale Collection. She loves to hear from her readers, and you can contact her at jenni@authorjennijames.com.

STAY IN TOUCH WITH JENNI JAMES

****

Visit authorjennijames.com
to learn more about Jenni,
read interviews and reviews,
and get all the details on upcoming titles.

****

Become a fan on **facebook**
Author Jenni James
The Jane Austen Diaries

Follow her on **twitter** Jenni_james

Send her an ✉ email jenni@authorjennijames.com

TAYLOR ALWAYS GETS WHAT HE WANTS—UNTIL NOW.

Chloe Elizabeth Hart despises the conceited antics of the popular crowd—or more importantly, one very annoying, self-possessed guy, Taylor Anderson, who seems determined to make her the president of his fan club! *As if!* Every girl in the whole city of Farmington, New Mexico, is in love with him, but he seems to be only interested in Chloe.

This modern high school adaptation of *Pride and Prejudice* is a battle of wits as Chloe desperately tries to remain the only girl who can avoid the inevitable—falling for Taylor.

SOMETIMES A GUY IS EVEN BETTER THAN YOU IMAGINED . . .

The Russo family and Seattle, Washington, are no match for Claire Hart and her savvy knowledge of all things vampire-related. Thanks to her obsession with the Twilight series, if there is anyone who would know a vampire when she saw one, it's Claire. And she's positive totally hot Tony Russo is a vampire—she just has to prove it!

In this modern retelling of Jane Austen's *Northanger Abbey*, follow Claire's hilarious journey on her first summer adventure away from home, where she learns everything isn't what it seems, and that in some instances, reality is way better than anything she could ever find in a book.

WILL HE TAKE HER BACK, OR FLING HER ASIDE LIKE SHE DESERVES?

Three years ago, Amanda made the biggest mistake of her life—she let her friends persuade her to reject the guy she loved. They were convinced he was a loser and wasn't good enough for her.

Now Gregory's back in Farmington . . . taller, stronger, hotter than ever, and worth millions. Those gorgeous girls who snubbed him before are now falling at his feet—and he's enjoying every moment of it.

Can he see past the pain Amanda caused him and give her a second chance? Or will she forever regret losing the only guy who truly loved her?